Nick could not allow this conversation to end up in her bed.

Jane reared back, warning him off. "It was a mistake."

"Agreed," he said, although her feeling that way, too, drove disappointment into his heart. "But it was still amazing."

She blushed that blood-stirring blush. "It shouldn't have happened."

"Jane, I won't deny that I'd like nothing better than to pursue whatever this attraction is between us." *So much so, it's killing me not to kiss you right now.* "But I'm sorry I took advantage."

She dragged a hand through her hair, ran her tongue over her lips, and looked at her bare feet. It took every ounce of will power in him not to take back his words, not to touch her. She glanced up, contrition in her eyes. "It wasn't all your fault."

Acclaim for the Big Sky Pie Series

DELICIOUS

"*Delicious* deserves four big, yummy, juicy stars...Lee gives her readers mesmerizing descriptions of baking pies, wonderful characters, and a fresh take on love."
—RandomBookMuses.com

"Five Big Sky blueberry pies for this fabulous romantic page-turner...You'll want to savor each slice of this scrumptious series."
—TheBestReviews.com

"Fast-paced and engaging...a wonderful addition to Lee's heartwarming series."
—BookReviewsandMorebyKathy.com

DELECTABLE

"For a fun, light, and entertaining read about second chances, don't miss *Delectable*."
—HarlequinJunkie.com

"I found *Delectable* so refreshing!...True love and homemade pies made this totally delectable!"
—RandomBookMuses.com

Delicious

Also by Adrianne Lee

Delectable
Delightful
Delicious
Decadent

Delicious

Adrianne Lee

FOREVER

NEW YORK   BOSTON

Forever

Hachette Book Group

237 Park Avenue, New York, NY 10017

www.HachetteBookGroup.com

Printed in the United States of America

Originally published as an ebook

First mass market edition: June 2014

10 9 8 7 6 5 4 3 2 1

OPM

Forever is an imprint of Grand Central Publishing.

The Forever name and logo are trademarks of Hachette Book Group, Inc.

The publisher is not responsible for websites (or their content) that are not owned by the publisher.

The Hachette Speakers Bureau provides a wide range of authors for speaking events. To find out more, go to www.hachettespeakersbureau.com or call (866) 376-6591.

For all my Montana friends—you know who you are—and all the years we summered together near Flathead Lake.

Acknowledgments

THANK YOU:

Larry and Spooky—for making me laugh when I most need it.

Bette Jo Carlton—for teaching me, when we were both young brides, how to make a pie crust.

Anne Martin—for being willing to meet me on a moment's notice for plotting help.

Jami Davenport—who understands what makes a real hero sexy.

Gail Fortune—my fabulous agent.

Alex Logan—for keeping my stress at bay and everything else you do for me that I'm not even aware of.

Delicious

Chapter One

~~~

"When it comes to men, Janey, your mama is as flaky as the crust on my blueberry pie."

Her grandmother's words taunted Jane Wilson as she stared at her ringing cell phone. The screen showed a stunning, amber-eyed brunette, former Miss Montana, every bit as beautiful now as the day she'd been crowned. Rebel Scott, aka her "flaky" mother. If Jane could, she would detour around the coming evening like a highway accident and just avoid the whole mess. But somehow she always got sucked into the mama-drama.

"I didn't forget, Mom," she answered, juggling the phone and two pie boxes into her Jeep. This month's specialty at Big Sky Pie just happened to be Jane's specialty, blueberry pies with buttery crusts that melted on your tongue. "Just leaving the pie shop now."

Her mother laughed, a sound as melodious as perfectly tuned chimes. "Oh, good. I was afraid..."

That I'd changed my mind? That I wasn't interested in meeting your latest fiancé, a man whose name you won't even tell me? Jane prayed for the courage to do what she meant to do tonight; after all, it was for Mom's own good. "I have the address and the pies. I'll see you around six."

If I don't chicken out by then.

If I can find something to wear, Jane thought, half an hour later as she shuffled through her closet, keeping in mind her own preference for comfortable clothes and her mother's idea of dinner-appropriate attire. Her mother insisted that she had passed her grace and beauty on to Jane, as well as her singing talent, and that Jane should be competing in beauty contests. *Wishful thinking.* Jane knew better. She would never be a "Miss" anything. On a one-to-ten beauty scale, she was a solid seven. She'd inherited her dad's strawberry blond curls and aqua eyes, and Grandma Wilson's tendency to gain weight just passing by a refrigerator. Could she have chosen a worse profession than pastry chef? Jane smiled. The fact was, the career had chosen her. She'd been baking pies for as long as she could remember.

If getting married was her mother's passion, baking pies was Jane's. Not men or dating. Growing up with a serial-bride mother had soured Jane on love. She didn't need a man to define or complete her. She had a calling.

A calling that was not doing her figure much good, she realized, as she tried on her black sheath and leopard heels. The effect was a longer, leaner look, as chic as Jane ever got, and pulling her hair back in a French braid would highlight the one asset she shared with her mother, her cheekbones, but the image in the mirror showed the dress hugging in a few wrong places, thanks to the fifteen pounds she'd gained at cooking school. The sheath was her only option, however, and it would have to do.

Not that she was likely to gain an ounce tonight given the knot filling her stomach, a knot that grew worse as she soaked in a bubble bath, and after, as she gave herself a pedicure. She might be a mess inside, but she was determined to *look* put together.

* * *

"Love is like-a my cottage cheese pie, Nickola. Some never take a taste, but those willing to give a try...they in for a big delish-a surprise-a." Anna Taziano's advice seemed to pour from the car speakers, startling her grandson Nick as he hit the city limits of Kalispell, Montana. Just back from a business road trip, Nick was suffering the sting of yet another romantic split and longing for some good, old-fashioned, family comfort. So much so apparently that he was receiving it from the great beyond.

He sighed with regret. Granna's loss was always with him like a bruise that wouldn't ease. He missed her old-world wisdom, her counsel. *What would she say if she were still here?*

Stalled at a red light, he envisioned her standing in her farmhouse kitchen, her solid little body encased in its proverbial apron, gray hair twisted into a knot on her head as she shook her wooden spoon at him and *tsk*ed. "What I tell-a you, Nickola? You must make-a the sincere, from-a the heart."

Nick smiled wryly, thinking this was probably the root of the problem. His love life had never been sincere, or from the heart. More like a series of hookups based on convenience, the *L* word never entering into the equation. A by-product of his business. He didn't have time for any long-term, serious relationships, so there had been no Ms. Right's in his life, just a lot of Ms. Right Nows.

The light went green, and Nick turned onto a side street, then circled into an alley two blocks over and into his garage. Though the main office for his advertising company, Adz R Taz, was housed in this downtown Kalispell building, Nick traveled a corridor from Spokane to Billings to Cody, and all places in between to work with customers, setting up or improving their advertising campaigns. The result of so much traveling was that he met some interesting women. Mostly through the lens of his camera. Mostly too-thin models.

And he'd been fried more times than a digital image sensor.

It was getting old. Hell, he was getting old. And lonely. If he wasn't careful, he would end up like his dad—an aging workaholic with no personal life. Nick would give anything if his dad could find someone he loved the way he'd once loved his second wife, but the bitch had soured his dad on marriage and skewed Nick's view of it as well. She and her obnoxious little girl, a real pain in the ass.

Nick grabbed his bags from the back of his SUV and started up the stairs to the second-floor loft where he lived and worked. His cell phone rang as he unlocked the door and shoved the bags inside. Still in ad-man mode, he answered without looking at the screen. "Nick Taziano."

"Nicky!" His dad's booming voice instantly lifted Nick's spirits. Damn, he missed his old man. He and Nick moved to Las Vegas after the divorce. His dad still lived there, but Nick had returned to Montana a couple of years ago, where a man could fill his lungs with fresh, crisp air and let his creative juices flow.

"Dad, I was just thinking about you." Nick shut the loft door and glanced around. Everything looked as he'd left it. The loft was wide open with brick walls, high ceilings, exposed ductwork, and warehouse-sized windows. His work area took up one end wall and consisted of a wraparound counter/desk combo that held his computers, printers, and cameras. "Just walked in the door from a road trip. How're things shaking in Sin City?"

"Wouldn't know," his dad said.

What the hell did that mean? Nick set the briefcase on the work counter, then carried his duffel bag into the bedroom and dropped it on the bed, frowning. "Don't tell me you've finally taken a vacation."

"Even better."

Nick pulled his toiletry bag from the duffel and went to the bathroom. A glance in the mirror confirmed a need to shower and shave, but right now, he wanted a beer. He headed back into the main room to the mini-fridge, mulling over what his dad considered even better than a vacation. Romeo Taziano loved cars. Old, new, hot rod, classic. An ace mechanic by the time he was twenty, outgoing and honest, he soon owned an auto repair shop, and when they moved to Vegas, he bought a Rolls-Royce limousine and started Black Tie Limo. Over the past fifteen years, he'd acquired Town Cars, Cadillacs, Hummers, stretch limos, and party buses, becoming one of the city's premiere transportation services. The only thing Nick could think of that his dad would consider better than a vacation was a staycation chauffeuring some world-famous movie star around town. "Congratulations."

His dad laughed. "Tell me that after you've heard my news."

"Okay. I'm all ears."

"I sold the business and retired."

Nick's fingers froze on the twist cap of the beer bottle as the impact of this registered. Romeo had meant for Nick to take over the business when he retired, but Nick didn't share his love of cars, and the frenetic energy of Vegas got on his nerves, stifled his creativity. Still, why would Dad suddenly sell out and retire? He wouldn't. It made no sense...unless...God, was he ill? Seriously ill? "Dad, are you feeling okay?"

"Never better, son."

Relief flooded Nick, but it didn't answer his questions about his dad's sudden retirement, and his dad wasn't offering explanations. "I figured you'd keel over behind the wheel of the Rolls before you ever retired."

"Yeah, I kind of thought that might be my fate, too. But things change."

Nick took the beer to his bedroom, sank onto the bed, and kicked off his shoes. "Why is this the first I'm hearing about this? What the hell changed?"

"A lot. In a pretty short time span, too. Look, it's more than we can discuss over the phone—"

"Like hell. I'm not letting you go until you've told me everything."

"I was hoping you'd say that." There was a pause, then his dad said, "I sold my place in Vegas and bought a condo here."

"Here? As in Kalispell?"

"Yep. On Flathead Lake."

"No shit?" Nick gave a whoop of joy. "Then you're in town?"

His dad laughed. "Moved in this weekend. Wanted to be settled before I told you."

More likely, he hadn't wanted to ask Nick to help him move since he knew Nick had a solidly booked work schedule. Like father, like son. As he took down the address, Nick said, "Hey, I know this place. I did their brochure ads and some online stuff. Dad, I can't wait to see you." They'd had too little time together these past few years. "We have lots of catching up to do. Let me unpack and wash off the road, then I'll head that way."

"Sounds great. Bring your camera. I'm throwing a little get-together, and I'd like to commemorate this new phase of my life."

He wouldn't be having his dad to himself? Normally that might disappoint Nick, but given his dad had moved to town, there would be plenty of father-and-son time. Nick had only one reservation. This new phase might bore the socks off his type A personality father. He didn't want to rain on his dad's parade, especially when he sounded so cheery, but it had to be said. "Are you sure you're going to have enough to do with your days now?"

"Well, that's another little surprise I've been saving for you."

Nick wasn't sure he could take another surprise and braced for bad news. "What?"

"You might want to sit down for this one, pal." His dad laughed.

"I am sitting down."

"Your old man is getting married."

Nick's mouth dropped open, but the shock quickly spun to delight. Yes, it was happening pretty damned quickly, but after a two-decade drought, fast seemed almost called for. "That is fanfuckingtastic! Who is this lucky lady?"

His dad was laughing again. "You'll meet her tonight. Party starts at six p.m. Champagne and dinner on me."

Nick hung up, grinning. "Well, Granna, it looks like your son, Romeo, took your advice." He was taking a chance on love. Nick hoped his dad was in for one "big delish-a surprise-a."

* * *

At five forty-five, Jane found herself maneuvering through Kalispell's late afternoon rush hour traffic, summer sunshine a glare on the windshield. A warm breeze swept in through the open Jeep windows and across the pie boxes on the passenger seat, blowing the sweet perfume of freshly baked blueberry pie past her nose. Instead of comfort in the familiar aromas, Jane found only disquiet. Why wouldn't her mother tell her who she was marrying?

Probably worried I'll Google him. Like last time. And the time before that. But wasn't it a daughter's obligation to look out for her mother when the mother didn't seem to ever look out for herself? Of course it was.

Once Jane reached the outskirts of town, she glanced at the GPS app on her phone, checking the directions. Five miles farther on, she spied the sign for Buffalo Ridge hanging from a massive stone arch and pulled onto a blacktopped drive that led down to a wide-open parking area. Jane's gaze went to the four-story building that stood on the edge of Flathead Lake. The exterior seemed to have been carved from the natural, gigantic boulders and Douglas fir prevalent along the lakeside, the visual effect something between a grand hotel and a mountain lodge.

The interior continued the natural theme and yet offered a sense of grandeur in the slate floors and rich decor. There was even a doorman and security. She gave the doorman her mother's name, was checked off his list of expected party guests, and given directions to the condo.

Balancing the pie boxes on top of each other, Jane headed for the bank of elevators, her gaze on the wall of windows that showed views of the lake and manicured flower beds that swept right to the water's edge. The sheer beauty captured her attention... until the heel of her pumps caught on a groove in the slate flooring. She wobbled, but righted herself, clutching tighter to her packages. A fine mess she'd be if she ended up on her butt in the lobby of her mother's new digs, blueberry pie splattered everywhere.

She concentrated on putting one foot then the other solidly on the floor, trying to ignore the splendor of her surroundings and failing. How much did it cost to live in a place like this?

Leave it to Mom to snag another wealthy Romeo. A chill slipped down Jane's spine and triggered an old anger. A man named Romeo had caused the breakup of her parents' marriage almost fifteen years ago. To this day, Jane had never forgiven him. She'd lived a year with him as her stepfather and his evil son as a stepbrother. She shuddered.

If not for *that* Romeo, her mother wouldn't be flaky when it came to men, or have ended up marrying every Romeo since who crossed her path. That man ruined her mother's life. *And mine.*

Jane grappled with the pie boxes, her purse, and cell phone as she stepped into the private elevator and pushed the penthouse button. Just as the door started to close, Tall, Dark, Drop-Dead Gorgeous hurried inside. She reared back and almost dropped the pies, her face heating with alarm.

He reached out to steady her, his cologne stealing through her, a citrusy scent that smelled like...key lime pie? He had a husky, sensuous voice. "Sorry, I didn't mean to startle you."

His deep-dimpled grin reached his warm chocolate eyes, sending a curl of heat through her middle. She couldn't find her voice. She just nodded.

He turned toward the control panel, humming, seeming to be too happy about something to notice her discomfiture. She wished she could find something happy in this situation, wished that she were only a party-goer and not the daughter of a woman who'd lost her last marble.

As the elevator began its ascent, he moved into the corner opposite her and did what men seemed wont to do whenever a woman crossed their paths...checked her out from head to toe. The already too-tight dress seemed to shrink under his assessing eye, making her more aware than ever of how the fabric hugged her curves. A burn, not unlike desire, flamed through her, but of course, it wasn't desire. She didn't even know this guy, or want to know him.

His gaze finally reached her face, his expression belonging to that of a champion poker player. He gestured to the boxes she held. "Big Sky Pie, huh? Best pies in town, I hear."

"They are," Jane said, her voice almost a whisper. As

much as she appreciated the compliment, she didn't tell him that she was the pie shop's new pastry chef. The fact that she'd landed this job and got to work every day in the kitchen of her dreams was still such a wonder to her that she didn't want to jinx it by bragging about it. Besides, sharing that tidbit might encourage conversation, and she didn't feel like talking to anyone. Except her mother.

She braced as the elevator stopped, noting from the corner of her eye that he'd taken an expensive-looking camera from his jacket pocket. He slipped the shoulder strap onto his fine-looking shoulders. He must be the photographer for the party. The door slid open, and music and voices hit them in a wave; the party was already under way and promised to be a lively one.

Jane stayed just inside the elevator, a severe case of cold feet washing over her. This was not the time or place for a serious discussion with her mother. Bad idea. She shouldn't have come. She reached to push the down button, but Gorgeous Elevator Guy snatched the pie boxes. "I've been here before. Follow me. The kitchen is this way."

Reluctantly, she trailed after him, wondering where her mother was and who all these people were. A dinner party, she'd said. *Why didn't I ask how many guests were expected?* Two pies would not feed this crowd. The entry tile gave way to a sleek hardwood and a sleeker kitchen. Caterers were preparing hors d'oeuvres on serving trays. Gorgeous Elevator Guy placed the pie boxes on the counter.

She thanked him for the help, but he didn't move off. "I want to see what's in those boxes."

"Blueberry pies." *My specialty.* She removed the pies from the boxes and set them on the counter. The filling, sweet and gooey, poked through the scored top. The crusts were golden brown and clustered with tiny, pie-dough hearts, a sugary glaze drizzled over the tops.

"Wow." He whipped out his camera and took a photo, then turned his lens on her. She raised her hands, warding him off. He grinned, lowering the camera away from her face, but not taking it completely off her. "Camera shy, huh?"

"Something like that."

His camera flashed again. "Great shoes."

This time, Jane couldn't help but return his smile. She thought the shoes were great, too.

She thanked him and was about to attend to cutting the pies when she spied a ghost from her past. Was she mistaken? No. He was older, gray threading his ebony hair, but it was definitely one of her former stepfathers. The one who broke up her parents' marriage. Romeo Taziano. "No, no, no..."

What was he doing here? Coming toward her as though he recognized her after all these years? He may have changed a little, but she had changed a lot. Every instinct she had seemed to cry, "Run. Hide." But there was nowhere to hide, and he was between her and the elevator. She reached for Gorgeous Elevator Guy. "Quick, kiss me."

His black eyebrows arched. "What?"

She didn't have time to explain. She threw her arms around him and pulled him to her, her gaze pleading with his. He stopped resisting, touching his soft, firm lips to hers. A jolt of pleasure unlike any she'd ever experienced flashed through Jane. *Oh, my, key lime pie never tasted so good.* The room seemed to spin away, the voices disappeared, and the music softened to a waltz, until the only thing she heard or felt or was aware of was the man whose arms were around her.

The magic moment snapped at the words, "Well, son, it looks to me like you've found a special lady, too."

Jane recognized Romeo's voice, but who was he calling son? She broke the kiss with Gorgeous Elevator Guy, finding herself a bit breathless. Her hated former stepfather was not looking at her, but straight at Gorgeous Elevator Guy. He released her and spun to greet Romeo with that dimpled smile and a bear hug. "Dad."

Shockwave upon shockwave rolled over Jane. Nick Taziano? She'd been kissing her one-time, despised stepbrother, the Tazmanian Devil? *Oh, my God.* She bolted for the elevator, darted inside, and punched the button to close the door.

Her mother's face flashed against the narrowing slit. "Jane?"

And then, Nick Taziano's voice reached her, sounding as shocked as she felt. "That was Jane the Pain?"

Chapter Two

"Seriously? Your mother is remarrying one of your ex-stepfathers?" BiBi Henderson, Jane's assistant pastry chef, asked, echoing Jane's ongoing shock. A mini-dynamo with Miley Cyrus hair and round, baby blue eyes, BiBi was in charge of making the fillings, while Jane made the crusts. She glanced up from the stemmed and rinsed blueberries she was stirring into a huge bowl of cinnamon, sugar, flour, and lemon zest. They were the only two employees in the pie shop at this predawn hour. "And I thought my family was complicated."

Still reeling from the identity of her mother's latest flame, Jane gave no thought to the wisdom of venting about her personal dilemma to her assistant. It was either this or her head would explode.

Jane stood across the marble worktop from BiBi, buffeted by cream-colored French Country cabinets, fighting the urge to pommel a mound of dough. "Not just one of her exes, but the one who broke up her marriage to my dad."

"Ouch," BiBi said. She and Jane were both daddy's girls. Jane knew she could do no wrong in her daddy's eyes. BiBi, however, constantly sought her daddy's approval, attention, or affection. Jane didn't know which. She wasn't sure BiBi knew either. What BiBi did know was that her daddy expected her to be the head pastry chef in this pie shop. Second place wasn't good enough. Given that, it constantly surprised Jane that BiBi didn't strive harder to improve her pie-baking skills, or at least show some eagerness to learn.

She felt BiBi's curious gaze. "Is that why you were here like an hour and a half early this morning?"

"I couldn't sleep," Jane said. Normally, their workday started at 4:30 a.m. Today, however, Jane had gotten a head start. BiBi arrived to find all eight ovens filled with baking pies, the kitchen awash in peach and apple scents. Jane was still too keyed up to feel the exhaustion, but she knew it would hit her hard later. Four pie pans with bottom crusts awaited the blueberry mixture. The top crusts were in the Sub-Zero to keep them chilled until she was ready for them.

Soothing country guitar music floated through the fragrance-rich kitchen and plied its magic until she could breathe again, until the stone against her heart pressed less heavily. Nothing calmed Jane's jangled nerves like baking pies…especially here, at Big Sky Pie. Located directly across the street from the Kalispell Center Mall, Molly McCoy's pie shop had opened eight weeks ago and offered pies, tarts, and cobblers that could be bought to take home or consumed on the premises in the café. The hours accommodated dessert-seeking customers: 10 a.m to 8 p.m.

"I don't know what my dad is going to say when he hears the news," Jane said, thinking out loud.

"Oh," BiBi said, making the word sound like a heart-break. "Wait, I thought you said your dad has been happily married to his current wife like forever?"

"Yeah, well, he might say it seems like forever, but I'm not sure he's all that happy." Jane brushed flour from her hands. Though they had never discussed it, she suspected her dad, Eddie Wilson, regretted his haste in marrying a second time. After the split from Jane's mother, he used to walk through his car dealership like a lost soul. She hadn't fully understood at the time, but once she was older, she realized that her stepmom—his office manager, Vicky Stivey—had taken advantage of his vulnerability, latching on to him while the ink was still drying on his divorce decree. Vicky wasn't a beauty like Jane's mother, but she was crazy about Eddie, had been since high school, and that was what his bruised ego needed at the time. "My stepmom is definitely devoted to Dad, but in a kind of smothering way. He's taken up golf and fishing and even hunting."

"Anything she doesn't want to participate in, huh?" BiBi shook her head and laughed. "Relationships are exhausting. I'm starting to think it would be better to find a guy on a website dating service. At least you'd be guaranteed to have things in common...if he didn't lie on his status. Or post someone else's photo."

"No thanks." Jane only had to look at her parents to know she was never getting married. Flaky Mom. Miserable Dad. "I don't think anything my mother does these days will surprise Dad." Or anyone else who knew her. "I just thought this might stir up unpleasant memories." *Like it has for me.*

"So how many times did you say your mom's been married? Four, five..."

Jane sighed. "This will be her seventh."

"I'm not sure it counts as seven since she's remarrying someone she wed before."

"It counts."

Jane transferred the blueberry mixture into the four pie shells, dotted unsalted butter on top, then retrieved the first top crust from the Sub-Zero. One of the keys to good pie crust was keeping the dough as cold as possible during the process.

BiBi said, "Wow, I hate to say it, but your mom sounds just like that actress...what was her name? Elizabeth Taylor."

"Her marriages don't last as long as some of Liz's did." Jane affixed the top crust on the first pie, trimmed the excess dough, and crimped the edges. "One was a few days."

"Yikes." BiBi placed the pie into the Sub-Zero, where it would need to stay for about half an hour. "Serial bride."

"Exactly." Jane nodded. She repeated the top crust

routine with the second pie, working quickly as she talked. "Planning that wedding took over a year."

"Wow." BiBi walked to the windows above the sink and began opening the blinds. Morning sunlight swept into the kitchen, bright and full of energy, promising another sweet June day. Perfect wedding weather. "Well, if your mom needs a local wedding planner, I have a friend—"

"My mom is a wedding planner. A very successful one. I thought when she took up that profession after husband number three that it would satisfy whatever itch she has to keep getting married—since obviously it's the wedding planning, not being married, that she loves. Turns out, she loves planning her own weddings best of all."

"Well, look at the positive." BiBi pulled out some pans that she would position under the pies to catch any bubbling juices as they baked. "If she's marrying someone who lives in Kalispell and she takes months to plan the wedding, you'll have the time to talk her out of going through with it."

Jane hadn't thought of that. "I was going to try and start doing that last night…before I even knew who her fiancé was."

"Total ambush." BiBi began stemming and rinsing another flat of blueberries. "See, this is why I don't like surprises. It's like Stacy and Clinton showing up at a party you're attending with cameras in your face, telling you that your family and friends think your taste in clothing sucks, and making you decide then and there if you want a head-to-toe makeover. Seriously. I would kill my friends and family as soon as the cameras shut down."

Jane finished the third pie. Last night was not some TV fashion show...though there had been a camera. She blushed remembering Nick and his camera, photographing her feet, his comment about her shoes. "Uh, *What Not to Wear* is not quite the same thing that went down last night." Jane suspected BiBi watched too much reality TV. She seemed to have a fascination with Hollywood and celebrities.

"Oh, God, you're right." BiBi drained the blueberries in a colander and then poured them into a large ceramic bowl. "It's more like someone inviting you to a fancy restaurant in order to break up with you. They figure you won't make a scene with all those strangers in the room."

"Yeah," Jane said, "like that...without the breakup part." If her mother wanted to get back with Romeo, why had she decided it would be better to spring that surprise in front of a roomful of strangers? *And if I'd been warned ahead of time, I wouldn't have accidentally kissed my ex-stepbrother...ewww.* Though recalling the shockwaves of desire that had rocked through her when the Tazmanian Devil's lips were locked with hers, Jane supposed that the kiss hadn't been exactly "ewww," more like "yumm." If she were honest with herself, she'd admit that that had been bothering her almost more than her mother remarrying Nick's father.

How could she have enjoyed kissing the Devil? What

did that say about her? Was she as loony as her mother? No. She wasn't. She had the good sense to know that she didn't want anything more to do with Nick Taziano. Ever.

BiBi broke into her thoughts. "You know, though, it is kind of romantic that your mom and this guy have reconnected. It's like they were meant to be."

Jane's fingers pinched too tightly on the edge she was crimping and broke off a chunk. She swore under her breath, glancing sharply at her assistant. "You think I should be happy for my mom?"

"Well, yeah, maybe."

God, this was the same reaction she'd gotten when she spoke to her best friend last night. It was like no one understood how wrong this was. She bit back the urge to scream and forced herself to keep a gentle touch on the rest of the edge she was crimping, when what she'd rather do was ball the dough and toss it at BiBi's clueless noggin.

Think of something pleasant, anything but your mother. In response, her mind instantly conjured up Nick and the kiss. She groaned softly. She did not want to think about Nick, or what a gorgeous hunk he'd grown up to be, or how she'd reacted to that damned kiss.

Still, if her mother went through with her marriage plans, avoiding Nick altogether would be impossible. At least he didn't know where she worked. And even if he should show up at Big Pie Sky someday, she was unlikely to encounter him; working in the kitchen meant that she seldom saw customers. Just staff. That suited her to a tee. Her mother always seemed to embrace the limelight of center stage while Jane preferred the wings, seeing, listening, unseen, unheard.

BiBi brought a clean bowl to the work counter, measured the appropriate portions of sugar, flour, cinnamon, and lemon zest, then retrieved the drained blueberries and added them to the mixture, stirring gently. "Have you spoken to your mom since last night?"

"By the time I reached my car, she was phoning, but I didn't answer. I was too upset. I'd already run out of the party in tears. She had to stay and deal with her guests. She didn't need me to make that harder than I probably already did." Jane hadn't meant to be a selfish bitch, or to hurt her mother's feelings, but she knew she might have made a scene if she'd stayed. If she talked to her mom while she was still trying to figure out how to accept this huge life change, she might say things she couldn't take back. It would be best if they spoke when Jane had calmed down and had a better handle on her emotions. "I finally texted her and asked her why."

"Really?" BiBi gaped with curiosity and seemed to lean halfway across the counter. "And what did she say?"

"She said she was happy." *And she hoped I would be happy for her, but all I see ahead is heartache.*

"See, she's happy. That's good. Yes?"

No. Not with that…that man. But Jane mumbled, "I suppose."

BiBi made a face, but said nothing more for several

minutes, just kept her head bent over the blueberries. "It's hard to believe."

"What? That I'd run out on my mom?"

BiBi laughed. "No. I was thinking out loud about blueberries. Did you know they're one of the best foods for you? They're good for your heart, your eyesight, and even prevent some brain diseases. We're doing a public service making this our pie of the month."

Jane nodded, deciding not to mention the sugar and calories might offset some of the blueberries' superpowers. After all, pie was good for the soul, and if blueberries added a little more goodness, all the better. Jane beat an egg. Ten more minutes and she could score the blueberry pies, add the egg wash, and start them baking. She said, "We'll make some turnovers with the mixture you're making now."

"Sweet." BiBi licked her lips. "So I've been wondering about something. If your mother left your dad for this Romeo guy, and they were married for over a year, why did they split up that first time?"

The question took Jane by surprise, and her grip on the pie plate she was placing on a rack in the Sub-Zero wobbled, threatening to spill. She steadied it, then straightened and closed the refrigerator door. "I'm not sure." Actually, she had no idea whatsoever.

At the time, she hadn't cared; she was just glad the hellish stepfamily was over. She didn't ever have to see the Tazmanian Devil again. But as she thought about it now, Jane was suddenly very curious. It occurred to her that the reason the marriage broke up might provide a solid argument to convince her mother that remarrying Romeo was a bad idea. She applied flour to a marble rolling pin, smiling with renewed purpose as she started on the turnover dough.

* * *

Nick stood on the sidewalk on Center Street, the afternoon sun beating on his aching head as he took in the setting. Maybe work would get his mind off the shock of discovering his father intended to remarry the bitch who'd broken his heart fifteen years earlier. Drinking hadn't done the trick, just given him a pounding hangover. At the time, it had seemed the best way to put on a good face and say the right things. He would have rather followed Jane's exit, but he couldn't do that to his dad.

Jane the Pain. Imagine that little pain in the ass growing into a curvy beauty. His mind flashed on her image, the sexy dress, the hit-this pumps, the unexpected kiss. Heat raced through his blood. Damn. She was the second surprise of the night.

The kiss had left him fucking breathless. He hadn't reacted to a woman like that since . . . since . . . hell, since never. It was a first. He'd felt like his balls might burst for five full minutes after she'd left the building. Despite what was going on with his dad, Nick found himself thinking of Jane more and more through the evening, and later, he was haunted through the night by erotic dreams starring his ex-stepsister, the Pain herself.

He had to find her, had to find out if what he'd felt

was a fluke, or something real. But considering how Jane used to hate his guts, he doubted she'd share his enthusiasm for a test kiss or two...even though he'd swear she was as rattled by that sensuous moment as he was.

Nick's gaze settled on the sign over the shop he'd come to photograph, and his wayward thoughts scattered. Big Sky Pie. The place where Jane had purchased the pies she'd brought to the engagement party last night. His camera lifted into position, and through its lens, he focused in on the building. It looked much different than when his friend Quint McCoy had his realty office here. Had that only been three months ago? Wow. Nick had been on the road so much he hadn't had time to swing by here and even take a look until today.

This business was the brainchild of Molly McCoy, Quint's mother, and a tribute to the ingenuity of the American housewife. Nick took some wide-angle shots. The outside brought to mind Molly's specialty, bing cherry pie, the siding painted a rich ruby red with white awnings over bay windows and white-and-tan trim and lettering. It would make for great copy. Nick lowered the camera, ideas for the new ads Quint and Molly wanted cartwheeling through his mind as he stepped inside the shop. The fragrant scent of fresh-baked pie assailed him. What was that smell? Cinnamon? Sugar? Blueberries? He snapped his fingers. The pies Jane had brought last night. He hadn't eaten any. Didn't much care for Jack Daniel's and pie. Now he was sorry he hadn't foregone the booze for dessert. Very sorry. His mouth watered, and his stomach agreed; he needed a piece of that pie.

The camera was to his eye again as he snapped several frames, taking in the high-backed, private booths along one wall, the round tables scattered about the café, the warm ruby-and-tan hues, and the welcoming atmosphere. Soft country-western music twined with the murmur of conversation and the occasional clink of silverware against dessert plates as customers consumed the shop's scrumptious-looking offerings.

"Hey, Nick," Quint McCoy called, leaning out of the end booth and signaling him over. "Good to see you."

If Hollywood ever came calling, Quint McCoy might find himself with a modeling career or gracing the cover of *GQ Country* in his Dan Post boots, denim shirt, and blue jeans. Nick wasn't into guys, but he'd noticed his pal turned ladies' heads wherever they went.

"Finally got a haircut, huh?" Nick teased, though Quint's thick black mop still brushed his ears and collar.

"My favorite barber is back," Quint said, his blue eyes sparkling with the joy of having reunited with his beloved wife. He'd had a hell of a year, losing his dad, almost ending up divorced, and his mother's heart attack. Nick was happy for him.

"Speaking of Callee, where is she?" He'd expected Quint's wife would want to be in on this meeting after hearing that she'd designed the brochures and menus for Big Sky Pie.

"She's got her designer cap on elsewhere today,

something involving the remodel of our apartment and the plumber."

"Some apartment. I hear it's the whole upper floor of the old Municipal Building? That's huge."

"Yeah, it is." Quint smirked. "But, hey, I brought my other best girl."

"Seriously? Molly?" Nick peered into the booth, spying Quint's mother hunkered in the corner. A spry redhead with the same blue eyes as her son, Molly offered up a sly grin, looking much better than the last time he'd seen her, shortly after her triple-bypass surgery. That was over two months ago. "This is a great surprise. How are you doing?"

"Better every day, but I still run out of steam pretty fast," Molly McCoy said. "Quint, get Nick some coffee, and let's get this meeting started."

The men joined Molly, Nick setting his camera and iPad on the table. Nick took a sip of coffee and activated the tablet, positioning the screen so that both of his clients could view some of his packages. He addressed the pitch to Molly. "Quint mentioned you wanted a website and maybe some other types of advertising. Here are some samples of what I've done elsewhere, but before I do anything specific, I'd like some input from you."

"I appreciate that." Molly beamed at her son, patting his hand, then leaned toward Nick, keeping her voice low. "I'm not sure what works and what doesn't. That's your area of expertise. So what do you suggest would work best for us to really put Big Sky Pie on the Flathead County map?"

"You want to make a splash, huh?" Nick grinned.

"I do."

"Then I suggest a good Internet presence, a website and blog, even a Facebook account." Nick wasn't sure Molly could handle the manic pace of Twitter and decided not to suggest that today. It could cause more stress than was good for her. "It's called social networking and is a good way to catch the attention of folks who spend a lot of time online. Pie-eating people."

"I'm not all that good on my computer, but I guess if someone shows me what I need to do, I could probably figure it out."

"What about the blog? Are you up to doing that?"

"I'm not a writer, Nick. I'm a pie baker," Molly said.

"I can hire someone to do that."

"Oh, good. Meanwhile, I want you to taste this month's pie and get an idea of what we offer." Molly waved at the counter girl, who arrived a moment later with a slice of steaming blueberry pie à la mode, the crust sparkling as if it were drizzled over with a glittery sauce.

Nick inhaled, and the sweet aroma had him grabbing for his fork. He began a slideshow on the iPad for Molly and Quint to watch. "So these are some of the websites I've created. See if one of these is anything like what you have in mind."

He scooped a bite of pie onto his fork, and as soon as the sugary sweetness met his taste buds, he moaned. The crust was buttery and flaked apart on his tongue, the blueberries so delicate they seemed to dissolve against his teeth, and the vanilla ice cream rich, the perfect accompaniment. "Holy sh—, er, cow!" he exclaimed, horrified he'd almost cursed in front of Quint's mother. "This is amazing."

Molly beamed, though Nick knew that she had not made the pie. She said, "I'll pass along the compliment to our new pastry chef."

"After tasting this, I'd suggest playing up this Pie of the Month with comments from actual customers on the blog. And since this is now my new favorite place to eat, I'm going to have to add another hour in the gym to counteract the calories this job is going to add to my daily total."

Quint laughed and patted his flat stomach. "Tell me about it."

"I'll need to meet the staff," Nick said around another bite of pie à la mode. "Get shots of the kitchen and anything else that seems pertinent. As long as your pastry chef doesn't mind."

* * *

Except for her thick blond hair, Andrea Lovette, Big Sky Pie's assistant manager, reminded Jane of her mother. Not that she was flaky, but she'd taken some tough knocks along the way, yet somehow was not deterred from being attracted to guys that she should avoid—like the man she and BiBi were drooling over at the moment.

At first, she thought it might be their boss, Quint McCoy. He was show-stopping handsome with longish black hair, his eyes so blue a girl could drown in them, but he was happily married. Besides, Andrea had been his office manager before working at the pie shop, and though they were good friends, she didn't seem interested in Quint that way. So it couldn't be him.

Jane tried not to listen to what they were saying, which boiled down to what they'd like to do to the guy under discussion, or what they'd like him to do to them. But she couldn't mute their voices. She felt warmer by the minute, as if she stood too near a heated oven, as if the sizzling girl talk were scorching the kitchen walls of the pie shop and would soon set the whole block on fire.

Or maybe a pie is burning. The thought sent her scurrying to check, but all was well there, and she went back to preparing the dough mounds for tomorrow's pies. The aroma of butter and flour usually had a calming effect, but right now it did nothing to settle her nerves. She didn't want to think about sex or men or sexy men, but this talk brought back the kiss she'd shared with the Devil last night. A very sexy kiss. Damn it all. She couldn't get it out of her head. Couldn't get Nick out of her head.

"He has the deepest dimples, too." BiBi sounded like she might swoon.

Jane froze. Had she said dimples? No. It couldn't be. Dare she take a peek into the café? No. No. No. She forced her attention back to the dough in the food processor, pulsing it another time, then another. Try as she might to ignore her curiosity, though, it got the better of her. She asked Andrea, "Who are you two talking about?"

BiBi sighed. "One of Quint's friends."

"One of his best friends." Andrea spun toward Jane. "Nick...Taziano. Haven't you met him? Well, don't fret, you will. He's going to be doing some advertising for the pie shop."

Jane felt the heat drain from her face, and her knees seemed to lose every tendon, turning rubbery, but before she could drop to the floor, the door into the café swung inward, and Molly, Quint, and Nick entered the kitchen.

Another chill shot through Jane, followed quickly by a blush that heated clear to the tips of her ears. She hadn't looked in a mirror in hours. Her French braid had to be a mess. No makeup, flour and blueberry fixings clung to her apron and probably her face. She didn't care what Nick would think, but she didn't like her employers to see her in such disarray.

"Nick, this is our new pastry chef," Molly said. "Jane Wilson."

"Well, I'll be damned." Nick's husky voice forced her to meet his gaze. His amused gaze.

Jane didn't find anything amusing about this development. The heat in her face flowed upward like lava racing across her forehead and scalp. Somehow she found her voice. "Nick and I, er...we've...met."

She almost laughed at how lame that sounded. When she'd told BiBi about her former stepbrother and her mother's fiancé, she had not mentioned names. Thank God.

"Wow," BiBi said. "You don't look so good, Jane. Maybe I should finish making the dough today and you should go home. It's not like you haven't already put in your eight hours."

Jane stiffened. BiBi still harbored the mistaken belief that the head pastry chef job should have gone to her, despite her poor baking skills. She seemed to desperately need attention, even negative attention, and jumped at any opportunity to try to show Jane up. This was one instance when Jane would gladly let her—except then she wouldn't sleep again tonight worrying about how tough tomorrow's pie crusts would end up. She felt everyone waiting for her response, none more eagerly than BiBi. "No, no. I'm fine. A little headache is all. Nothing a couple of Tylenol won't cure."

She fled to the bathroom, grabbing her purse along the way. She closed the door, shut the lid on the toilet, and sat down, taking several deep breaths, muttering to herself, "Damn, damn, damn." She'd hoped Nick wouldn't ever discover where she worked, but then she hadn't realized that he was one of her boss's best friends or that he'd been hired for some ad campaign. Now not only did he know where to find her, but she'd be working with him. She cursed the unnamed powers that had brought him back into her life.

It's just for a while, a very short couple of days. Telling herself that didn't seem to help.

The reflection in the mirror appalled her. She looked washed out, flour on her face, and sure enough, her messy, unkempt strawberry blond hair had come loose from its French braid. She dug a comb and some makeup from her purse, washed her face, repaired her hairdo, and applied some mascara and lip gloss. Much better. She brushed off her working apron and opened the bathroom door.

Nick was there. He leaned toward her, his key lime scent reeling her in, and whispered, "We need to talk."

Chapter Three

Y ou are the last person I want to talk with," Jane whispered back. Nick was staring at her mouth intently, and her lips felt suddenly dry. Her tongue slipped across them, and a static charge seemed to jump through the air. If she touched him, she knew she'd feel a shock. Flustered, she skirted by him, put her purse back in the employees' closet, and strode into the kitchen, finding it empty. "Where did everyone go?"

"Quint took Molly home. She was pretty done in," Nick said, following her with his camera to his eye. "Andrea and the little brunette are cleaning up the café for the evening shift."

"Stop taking pictures of me." A trace of panic skipped through her. She didn't like sharing her domain, her comfort zone, with the Devil. Didn't like being photographed. Especially by him. He disturbed the balance, the normal sense of peace she felt here. "Why don't you leave? I have pie dough to finish."

"I don't have anywhere to go."

Jane did a slow burn. She could hardly toss him out of a pie shop owned by one of his best friends. "If you're going to stay, then no more photos."

"I promise to only focus my shots on what your hands are doing. Not on you."

It was as much of a compromise as she was going to get, and Jane knew it. Grappling with her distress, she pretended he wasn't there. She emptied the mealy-looking mixture from one of the food processors onto the marble counter, then gently worked the dough into a cohesive mound. Then she did another and another and another. Soon she didn't even hear the click of his camera, but she could feel his curiosity like a touch.

Nick asked, "What are those little flecks in the dough?"

"Bits of butter. It's what makes for flaky crusts."

"Ah, well, I can attest to the fact that your crusts are a delicacy."

The compliment pleased Jane in a way that receiving a five-star review from a food critic would, but since this compliment came from Nick, it was even better. And it was a first from him. She fought a smug smile as she patted the dough mounds with flour and placed them in plastic wrap. The fragrance of nearly finished blueberry pies saturated the air. Jane checked the timers, then caught Nick doing something he'd said he wouldn't do. "Are you taking pictures of me again?"

"It's for the advertising campaign."

"Ohhh, nooo." She raised a palm toward the lens as though warding off an intrusive paparazzo and carried the tray of wrapped dough mounds to the Sub-Zero. "I am not going to be part of that."

"Actually you are," he said, sounding enthused. "This is, after all, a pie shop, and from the blueberry deliciousness I just tasted, you are the main subject of interest in a lot of what I plan to use for the website and the blog."

Website? Blog? Jane froze, her gaze locking with his as he lowered the camera. Those deceptively warm chocolate brown eyes that she remembered so well, that expression. He was as serious as a head-on collision. Every cell in her body balked. No way in hell. She didn't like being the center of attention, ever, but being Nick's center of attention for hours or days or weeks would be unbearable. She'd lived that torture for a year as a kid. She did not intend to be subjected to it again.

What are you going to do then? Quit? Throw your dream job away on a tantrum? Run out like you did last night? Jane sobered. The idea that she would run whenever things got too much showed a whole new side of herself she didn't much like. She wasn't a coward, but running was cowardly behavior. As Grandma Wilson always said, "A picture is worth a thousand words of denial."

Nick grabbed her shoulder, startling her, and like last night, his touch sent a jolt of awareness through her, sexual awareness. Okay, she had to admit it. He'd grown into a deliciously handsome hunk who could cause a woman's heart to pound out of its chest, and she was not immune to the allure of the man. But she knew him. He might seem the perfect guy, but she could tell just by looking at him that he still had a heart as black as sin. She didn't trust that easy smile, those disarming dimples.

"If you keep scowling so hard, you'll give yourself a headache," he said, pulling her out of her thoughts. "I promise it won't be that bad, Jane. I'm serious. The camera loves you."

As if *that* were the point. He didn't get it. He never had, he never would. "I don't care."

Nick's eyes widened, and he gaped at her as if this was the first time any woman had ever said she didn't care whether or not she photographed well. Or maybe it was that no woman had ever refused to be photographed by him until now. He seemed truly dumbfounded. "You're joking, right?"

She shook her head and crossed to the sink to wash her hands, talking over her shoulder. "I don't own this shop. The focus of your campaign should be on Molly McCoy. On how she turned a lifelong love of making pies into a business. How, despite losing her husband and almost her life to a heart attack, she is still bringing her famous, prize-winning pies to the public."

Nick shrugged. "Of course that will be part of the history."

"Your photos should show the café, the kitchen, even the front façade of Big Sky Pie, which are all Molly's concepts. Photograph the display cases that hold the variety of desserts we offer, the pies, the tarts, the turnovers, the cobblers. Mention we serve ice cream and coffee." *In other words, do photos and copy of anything and everything, except me.*

"But don't you see?" he argued. "Part of Molly's success story is finding the right pastry chef to fill in for her while she recovers from heart surgery. Everyone is going to be curious about the person who bakes these incredible pies."

Jane had the oddest impression that he was the one who was interested in her. He was staring at her mouth again. She ignored the intimate shiver that swept through her. He was wasting his charm. She wasn't interested in him. Timers began buzzing. She dried her hands, then went to the ovens, donned oven mitts, and extracted turnovers and pies. The hot baking pans clinked as she placed the desserts on cooling racks.

Nick's camera kept clicking.

Yanking off the oven mitts, Jane growled, "Will you please stop?"

"Can't."

Anger twisted through her. "Nick, I understand your point of view, even appreciate it, but you aren't considering the larger picture, the possibility of a huge negative result if you focus on me."

"Such as?"

Jane lowered her voice. "Do you really want people curious about me? About us? About our insane parents? Have you even considered the harm that gossip could cause this shop?"

A light appeared in his dark eyes, something akin to

a hellfire flame. He smiled, and his dimples turned the whole look knee-shakingly sexy. "Gossip would probably bring a lot more people to the shop."

She huffed out a breath. "Yes, but for all the wrong reasons."

"You know what they say—even bad publicity is good publicity. My aim is to get folks into the shop by whatever means possible, and once they step inside and catch one whiff, they'll be goners. No one will leave without trying a slice of your heavenly pies—" He broke off, giving a finger snap. The camera was in her face again. "Yes, yes, that's the banner I'll use. The angel who bakes heavenly pies."

Jane wanted to finger-snap his ear. She groaned, ripping off her apron. She grabbed her purse and headed out the back door. "You're as insane as your father."

Outside, she registered the rumble of traffic as she hurried to her Jeep, but she was only marginally aware of the hot sun stroking her bare arms and flushed face. She worked with too many hot ovens every day to be daunted by a sizzling summer afternoon. She turned on the AC, plunked on sunglasses to hide the tears burning her eyes, and pulled out of the parking lot.

Was it just the day before yesterday that she'd been thinking her life could not be more perfect? What a difference a day or two made. One moment, she'd felt on solid footing, sure of herself and her next move, and then the ground transformed into a vast sea, and she stood on a surfboard riding a wild wave. She'd jump off if the water wasn't full of sharks.

Exhaustion had her yawning as she drove toward home. If she couldn't revert things to normal, then she'd settle for a slice of the leftover pepperoni pizza in her fridge, a glass of wine, a bubble bath, and shutting her mind the hell off. But her thoughts tumbled faster than Olympic gymnasts. How was she going to extract herself from Nick's ad campaign?

She released a small scream of frustration. She could complain to her bosses, insist that she be left completely out of it...and risk losing her job. Or she could cooperate, and maybe Nick would realize she was right about negative attention hurting the pie shop, and then maybe he'd focus the ad campaign on Molly. Like he should. Or maybe she would just have to tell him that she didn't like drawing attention to herself. She wasn't her mom.

Mom. What was she going to do about her? And how did she tell Dad? She needed to do that before he heard it elsewhere, but damn, she didn't have the energy to deal with that right now. She'd reached the limit of drama she could endure in any given twenty-four-hour period. She pulled into a parking slot at her apartment complex, and as she started to open her door, some jerk in an SUV pulled in beside her, almost blocking her in. The jerk was Nick. He'd followed her home? Damn him. If she'd even thought he might do that, she would have been on the lookout and lost him, or driven somewhere else.

She bailed out of the Jeep as he was climbing from his vehicle, exasperation oozing from her pores. "What?"

He said, "We need to talk."

"No, *you* need to talk. I don't. I've said what I had to say. I refuse to be the focus of your ad campaign, and no amount of talking is going to change my mind."

"About our parents."

Jane stopped in her retreating tracks. "Are you kidding me? There is nothing to discuss there either. Not with you."

"I take it you're no happier about them reconnecting than I am." He stood on the sidewalk four feet away, his hair mussed, his key lime scent floating on the breeze like incense. His white polo shirt and black chinos looked crisp, impervious to the boiling afternoon heat beating down on them.

Perspiration pooled between her breasts and at the small of her back, but it was the prickling on her fair skin that concerned her. A minute more without benefit of sunscreen, and she would be burned to a crisp. "Did you tell our parents how you felt last night?"

He looked away, then at his brown loafers, and finally at her, shaking his head. "I would have left, but you beat me to it. We couldn't both walk out. Besides, I didn't want to piss on Dad's happiness, delusional as it is."

Jane sighed, almost feeling sorry that he got stuck at the party last night. Almost. Secretly, mean-little-sisterly, she smiled to herself. "Maybe if all those other people hadn't been there..."

"Yeah, if I could have talked to Dad alone, I would have reminded him what a bitch your mother was to him. The biggest mistake of his life."

Bitch? Mistake? The words rankled Jane, rousing her

protective instincts as well as her hackles. She could call her mother names, but no one else better. "I would have made my mother see that your dad is the asshat who broke her heart and sent her down a path of self-destruction."

Nick's neck reddened. "My dad is the one whose heart was broken by your man-crazy mother."

Jane's fists curled at her sides. She'd never struck a man, but she was thinking about it now. "Your father is a home wrecker. He stole my mother from my father."

"Your mother goes through men faster than Taylor Swift."

Jane's next zinger died on her tongue. Much as she wanted to, she couldn't argue that point. At least Taylor had more sense than to marry any of the guys she dated and the savvy to turn each romantic disaster into another mega-hit single. Her mother's romantic disasters only hurt her self-esteem. She felt the sun burning her neck. "I'm not going to stand out here and argue with you."

"Then invite me in."

To argue some more? No thanks. "It's been a long day, and I'm beat."

She raced up the stairs to her third-floor, one-bedroom, end unit and rammed the key into the lock. Her cell phone rang. The photo on the screen showed her dad. She sighed. It seemed she couldn't dodge anything today. She bumped the door open, dropped her purse on the counter, and headed into her bedroom, the phone at her ear. "Hi, Dad."

"Janey baby, why didn't you tell your old man? Why did I have to read about it in the paper?"

Jane froze in the act of kicking off her Crocs. Oh, no. *Please don't let him have already heard. Please let him be talking about something besides my mother.* "In the paper?"

"Your mother. She's remarrying Romeo Taziano?"

Oh, God. Her heart dropped to her toes, and she sank to the bed. The engagement was in the newspapers? Already? She was heartsick. The farther along the wedding plans were, the harder it would be to deter her mom from this bad idea of a marriage. Jane began peeling off her chef pants and stained T-shirt, dropping them in a heap at her feet. "I'm sorry, Dad. I only found out myself last night."

"Then you should have called me right away. Or sometime today, at least. I don't like when my pals tell me something they assume I already know. Felt like a dumb shit."

"I'm so sorry." Lame, lame, lame. Jane mentally kicked herself for being too cowardly to phone him earlier in the day. She should have. She peeled off her bra and panties, donned her robe, and tied the belt. "I didn't have time all day, I swear."

Great. Now I'm lying to my dad.

"Well, I won't say anything bad about the guy," he said, implying he could say plenty. "But how are you feeling about it?"

In other words, nobody better hurt his little girl. Jane smiled. Her dad always had her back. "I'm not a card-carrying member of the Taziano Fan Club, if that's what you're asking."

She carried her dirty work clothes from the bedroom to the stacked washer and dryer in a closet near the bathroom. As she moved into the kitchen, a giant shadow loomed near the door. She startled. Nick! How? "I have to go, Dad. I'll call you later tonight, and we can talk more about it then, okay?"

She disconnected and glared at Nick. "What the hell are you doing in my home?"

"Not what I imagined from the outside," he said, assessing the apartment's space. "Tiny living room, huge open kitchen. Usually the opposite in these places. I suppose that's what you like about it, huh? The kitchen?"

She grabbed the nearest weapon at hand—a marble rolling pin she'd left on the counter—and slapped it against her palm. "How did you get in here?"

His expression went from bemused to big brother angry. He raised his hand. Her key ring dangled from his index finger. "You left these in the front door lock."

Her anger stalled as she frowned, trying to remember, but only recalled answering her phone to speak with her dad.

"Are you always so careless about your personal safety, Pain?"

The question relit her cooling jets, and she sent him a fiery look that would laser through an average man, but that didn't seem to singe the Devil, definitive proof of his hellish soul.

"It was like watching some version of *Scary Movie*…woman comes home, drops everything on the counter, and goes directly to her bedroom, starts stripping off her clothes, without first making sure she's locked her door and that she's alone in her apartment. All the while Freddy Krueger is about to jump from the closet with his knife and slash her to ribbons."

"You weren't hiding in a closet. You followed me inside. And I think you mean Jason. Freddy Krueger was from the *Nightmare on Elm Street* movies." Nick wasn't Freddy Krueger. He wasn't holding a knife, just her keys, but—wait! He'd seen her head into her bedroom and strip? What the hell? She clutched the neck of her robe, suddenly aware of how very naked she was beneath it and wondering how much he'd seen.

She snatched her keys, stuffed them into her pocket, and pointed to the door. "Get out."

He stood as though frozen to the fake hardwood floor. "Look, why don't you offer me a beer and we can hash this out?"

"We have nothing to hash out. Nothing."

"Our folks."

She shook her head, exasperation building in her. He was just as obnoxious as he'd been at twelve and thirteen. "Leave."

"Okay, I'll go, but first answer me this—since you're not a member of the Taziano Fan Club—do you want your mother to marry my dad?"

Spying on her? Eavesdropping? Was there no end to his evil deeds? Her hand curled tighter around the rolling pin, and her stance dared him to object to her opinion. "Not if your dad was the last man on earth."

The frown between his eyebrows disappeared, and a grin lit up his handsome face. "God, I was hoping you'd say that."

"I don't know what my mom is thinking." She set the rolling pin back onto the counter and tightened the belt of her robe.

"Maybe it's a menopausal thing."

Jane wondered if he had a brain in that handsome head. "She's only forty-one. While I'm sure that sounds ancient to you, it's too young for menopause."

Nick shrugged. "Wouldn't know. Lost my mom when I was nine, remember?"

Jane rolled her eyes. She was sure all things female eluded him—for which he likely blamed not having a mother through the critical years of his upbringing. That old sympathy card didn't work on her. She'd heard it too many times and knew it was just a ploy to excuse any bad behavior he didn't want to own up to.

"We can't let them go through with it." Sunlight glowed around his jet-black hair like a halo, adding to his innocent demeanor, but she recognized it as a trick of the light. He'd never ever been anything but devil through and through. "What are we going to do about it?"

We? He wanted to help her find a resolution? She'd felt like a lone warrior fighting a battle to save her mother from enemy forces, but now she was being of-fered assistance from the least expected source. Stress loosened its grip on her muscles. She wasn't alone, but she was surprised that she welcomed the company, given it meant forming an uneasy allegiance with her nemesis.

"I sure could use a cold beer," Nick said, his warm chocolate eyes staring at her lips as though what he really wanted was to ravish her mouth, reminding her that her reaction to that first kiss already had her running scared, reminding her that she was naked and vulnerable beneath her robe. She rechecked the belt.

Nick was dangerous on so many levels. Too many levels. He needed to leave, but instead of showing him the door, she found herself opening the refrigerator and pulling out a bottle of white wine. "No beer. Pinot blanc?"

He hesitated for half a second, then said, "As long as it's cold…" He slid onto a bar stool while she poured the wine into two long-stemmed goblets.

As she handed him a glass, she said, "Did you know the engagement announcement is already in the papers?"

"Seriously? Shit. I haven't read any online newspapers today." He pulled out his smartphone, and she assumed he was searching the Internet. "Damn, it's in the *Flathead Beacon* and the *Daily Interlake*."

"They're not wasting any time." She took a stool near Nick and caught him looking at her cleavage where the robe had parted slightly. She readjusted the collar, tightened the belt, and tugged the hem down over her bare knees. "I'm not sure what we can do to prevent this. I don't want to hurt my mom, just save her from another broken heart."

"I feel the same about Dad."

She drank her wine, the icy tang cooling her overheated brain as she waited for Nick to say something more, but he seemed to be waiting for her to speak. Finally, she broke the silence. "What exactly did you plan for us to do about this?"

"I was hoping you'd have some suggestions."

She rolled her eyes. "You came here wanting to hash this out, you said, so forgive me for thinking you probably had some plan or other in mind."

Nick shook his head. "Nope, but two heads are better than one, they say..."

She was too worn out to deal with him, with the whole situation, but even as she thought that, she suddenly remembered she had had an idea earlier in the day. "Nick, do you know why they broke up the first time?"

He ran a hand through his perfect hair, mussing it, making him even more gorgeous. She tried not to notice. He said, "What does that matter?"

"Answer me. Do you know?"

He frowned, shrugged, and shook his head. "I was thirteen. What did I care? Don't you know?"

"No. Haven't you ever asked in all these years?"

He offered a "why would I" expression. "No. Didn't you?"

"No." The wine began to take the edge off her nerves, pulling her to a calmer place. "But I think it's time we found out."

"Why?"

"So that we can remind them of whatever it was and hopefully jar them back to their senses."

"I knew you'd have an idea. You were always a conniving little...kid." His eyebrows lifted, followed by a smile of appreciation that showcased his dimples, but the backhanded compliment made her want to wipe that grin off his face.

He didn't seem to notice that he was rubbing her the wrong way. He never had read her well. He leaned toward her. "But how do we find out?"

Wasn't that obvious? "The best approach is usually a straightforward one. You ask your dad, I'll ask Mom."

He downed a gulp of wine. "I'm not sure that's a great idea. What if they compare notes and decide we're up to something?"

"Oh, good point." She sipped wine, thinking. "Then how will we find out?"

He snapped his fingers. "I'll bet your mother has a girlfriend or two she confided in."

"Of course she does. I should have thought of that." Names were popping into her head now, and she was sure she had a couple of phone numbers in her address book. Or somewhere in the house. Jane lifted her gaze to his, glad to finally have an avenue of inquiry to follow. She even found a smile. "Does your dad have guy friends he'd confide in?"

"Maybe. We moved to Vegas shortly after the divorce. Let me think about it."

"Do that." She drained her wineglass, realizing it was getting late—not for most folks, but for her. Her work hours defined her daily schedule. "Meanwhile, you need to go."

A bath was calling her name.

"But I'm not finished with my wine."

Jane snatched his glass and dumped the remains in the sink. "You are now. Good-bye, Nick."

She followed him to the door. He stopped just inside, glanced longingly at her mouth, and lower, offering up that sinful smile. As she reached to push him outside, he pulled her into a bold kiss, ignoring her struggles, releasing her a second later.

He grabbed her wrist, preventing the slap to the face she meant to give him. He shook his head. "If you're going to invite men into your apartment while half naked, there will be consequences."

"Invite?" she gasped and slammed the door on his devilish chuckle. She twisted the lock and put on the chain.

From the other side of the door she heard, "Still Jane the Pain."

Jane mumbled, "Damned straight."

Chapter Four

⌒

"Jane doesn't have a bad side," Nick said, staring at the enlarged digital shots he'd taken at the pie shop, marveling at how the camera—which usually revealed uncomfortable truths about his subjects—offered no such revelations about Jane. Whatever secrets she held were safe from his prying other-eye. For now.

"She bakes a great pie, too," Quint said, leaning over his shoulder to stare at the computer monitor. "Or did you even notice that?"

I noticed. Nick assumed his poker face and reached for his coffee. He'd noticed everything about Jane, couldn't get her off his mind; she'd even starred in his dreams. He'd figured kissing her last night would end the curiosity that their first kiss elicited. That had been a miscalculation on his part. He'd left there wanting more, more kisses, more touching, so much more…

"His mind wasn't on pie while he was taking these,"

Wade Reynolds said, weighing in on the photos. Wade and Quint were Nick's two best friends. They'd started holding weekly morning, bullshit sessions in Nick's loft to catch up. But today, Nick had invited them on an off-day to view his mock-ups for the Big Sky Pie advertising campaign.

Quint had brought a fresh-baked pie, another blueberry confection. With every bite he ate, Nick marveled that the pie's creator was Jane the Pain. She kept surprising him. Not all of the surprises were good, however—like her not wanting to be part of the advertising for the pie shop. He'd decided to show what he had in mind to Quint; let her boss make the decision. It would probably piss her off, but frankly, he didn't care. He couldn't let her stubborn refusal ruin the best possible angle for this promotion.

"Before you two yahoos go hooking Jane and me up romantically, there's something you need to know." He explained how he and Jane had known each other as children, and then said, "It was not what one might call a great time in our lives. We didn't bond as stepsiblings. Pretty much couldn't stand the sight of each other."

"But that doesn't seem to be a problem for you now," Quint teased.

"I don't know how I feel about her now." The lie rolled off Nick's tongue. He knew exactly how he felt about Jane. Annoyed. Attracted. Appalled. "But I'm fairly certain she still hates my guts."

"That should make this project interesting." Quint arched a sarcastic brow.

"She's very pretty." Wade was staring at Jane's photos. "Does she ever wear her hair down?"

Did she? Nick stared at her hair, wondering how long it was, the wayward curiosity surprising him almost as much as the twinge of jealousy that followed.

"I've only seen it up," Quint said. "But then I've only seen her at work."

"And that hairdo is probably preferred for working in a kitchen with food." Wade stirred sugar into his coffee. "Wonder how long her hair is."

Hearing his pal voice his own thought startled Nick. He glanced sharply at Wade. The possibility of his buddy being interested in Jane made him uneasy. What the hell? It wasn't like he had designs on her. That would be wrong on too many levels. *But kissing her and having erotic dreams about her is okay?*

He banned the little voice from his head. Why shouldn't Wade be interested in Jane? He could see where a lot of women might find the ruggedly good-looking, skyscraper-tall widower attractive. He was also one of the good guys, the straightest arrow Nick had ever met. Only two things about Wade might give a woman pause: his status as a single dad of a preteen daughter and the fact that he was buttoned up tighter than the fly of his faded Levi's.

Quint pointed to the computer monitor. "Can you print out some of these brochures and photos? Callee is having a staff meeting later today, and it would be great if she had these for show-and-tell."

"Already made you hard copies of it all." Nick

handed Quint a manila envelope. "I also included screen shots for the website. It's not available for public viewing yet. Just the working model for now. I need you and Callee to visit the site, give it a thorough going through, and then let me know your initial reactions, what you like, what you don't like, and what you might like to change, and then I'll keep tweaking until it meets your mama's one-hundred-percent approval, and then we'll go live."

"You know," Wade said, "maybe I need to hire you to build me a website and get some kind of advertising in place, now that I'm selling the cherry ranch and restarting my building business."

"I'll even write a 'satisfied customer' testimonial for the site." Quint patted Wade's back. "He and Callee have been working on our apartment, reshaping the footprint for that and the main retail level of the building. When this project is done, we'll be renovating some of the other old buildings Mama owns in town. Callee has come up with some amazing retail design ideas."

"That's great news," Nick said. Quint's mother owned the building Nick was living and working in. Quint's father had, throughout his life, purchased empty buildings in Kalispell, brought them up to code, remodeled to suit the era, and leased them for retail space. Quint had switched from the standard real estate brokerage to property development, carrying on his father's tradition.

Quint lifted his coffee mug in Wade's direction. "As

sorry as I am that cherry growing didn't work out for you, I'm glad you're back doing what you do best. You're an artisan, pal."

Wade shrugged off the compliment, but Nick could tell it pleased him. "The cherry ranch was Sarah's dream, not mine."

Which meant losing it hurt like hell, Nick thought, feeling bad for his buddy. Although Sarah had been gone for four years, it didn't mean the ache of her loss was any less. "Sorry, man."

"Yeah," Wade seemed to choke up, then shake it off. "Look, Taziano, I'm serious about this. Line me up for one of your ad blitzes. I don't need a blog. But a great website, some business cards, and brochures would do for a start."

"Hell, yes." Nick smiled. "Always glad for work that keeps me in town." Especially since the traveling he'd done the past couple of months had proven less lucrative than he'd hoped, and this would mean he didn't have to do another round of road trips for a few weeks.

"Speaking of staying in town, I hear your dad's moved back and that he's getting married," Wade said, his expression conveying that he thought this was great news.

"Well, that's the rest of the Jane and me story." Nick got up from behind his desk and strode toward the counter for another cup of coffee, half tempted to add a shot of whiskey to it. When he spun back to face his friends, they had moved to the conference table to finish their pie. Nick joined them. "Another reason she isn't too happy about this family reunion. The woman my dad is marrying, or should I say remarrying, is Jane's mother."

Quint's brows rose. "Oh, yeah?"

"Your ex-stepsister is about to become your stepsister again?" Wade seemed to catch on quicker than Quint.

"Exactly." Nick nodded. "Neither Jane nor I are happy about the upcoming unholy union."

Wade glanced up from his pie. "I thought you said your dad really loved this woman, and that she was the reason he hadn't married again since their split?"

Nick flinched as if his own words were darts hitting his back. "What I said was that the bitch who'd broken his heart had kept him from seriously dating anyone else or even considering marriage again."

Wade and Quint exchanged a look at his harsh tone.

Wade asked, "Then why is he remarrying her?"

Nick couldn't answer that. "I'm thinking senility."

Quint laughed. "Your dad's too young for that."

"Yeah, well, then maybe it was too many years in the Vegas sun."

Wade finished his pie and shoved the plate aside. "Have you told him how you feel?"

"Not yet. I'm not sure how to broach the subject. But I need to do it soon."

"Maybe you shouldn't butt in," Quint said. Obviously, he had a different slant on the subject of remarriage since he'd just renewed his vows with the wife he almost divorced. "I'm a true believer when it comes to second chances."

"I think you're just too close to the...pies to see the crust," Nick said, getting a grin from Quint.

"I'd give about anything to have a second chance with my Sarah," Wade said. "She might not have been everyone's dream girl, but she was mine."

Quint offered a sympathetic clamp on Wade's shoulder. "Sorry, pal."

"Me too," Nick said, meaning it, but also realizing neither of these guys understood his desperation to save his dad from the she-wolf's clutches. He gathered up the dishes and forks, putting them in the dishwasher.

"Mind if I take a piece of this pie home to Emily?" Wade asked Quint.

"Of course not. Take the rest of the pie if you like. I've got plenty more where that came from." Quint laughed at his own joke. "Speaking of the pie shop, I better get this ad stuff to the meeting. You did great, Taz. As always. Mama will be happy I recommended you."

With that, Quint left.

"Just get in touch when you have something you need me to look at for my ads," Wade said, heading out as well.

"Sure thing." Nick went back to his desk and stared out the window, the quiet of his studio closing in like a thick fog. He felt more alone than he had in a long time. No one to talk to who understood. His buddies hadn't come right out and said it, but the implication was there. *Be happy for your dad.* If only he could be. His dad may have forgotten the heartbreak Rebel caused him, but Nick hadn't.

He couldn't let her hurt his old man like that again.

* * *

Jane had not had a chance all day to phone any of her mother's friends in California. And now that all the day's pies were made, the dough readied for tomorrow, and the café at a lull, there was a staff meeting—which had already started. She'd only meant to take a ten-minute break at the mall, but she'd been distracted at the shoe store, and before she knew it, forty-five minutes were lost. She entered the back door, struck as always by the aromas of cinnamon, nutmeg, sugar, and flour. Especially flour. The scent and texture spoke to her. Dry or solid, it was her sculptor's clay.

She greeted the group seated on stools around the working counter, Andrea, BiBi, and Quint and Callee McCoy. As Jane joined the others, she eyed the papers splayed over the marble top. She caught glimpses of reds, whites, yellows, blues. "What are you all looking at?"

"Ad mock-ups for the website." BiBi's voice dripped honey as she cast Jane a surreptitious evil eye. "Seems someone is the star of the show."

She wanted to tell her assistant to put the green-eyed monster back in its box. BiBi was welcome to the limelight. Jane had no intention of being a star of this or any other advertising campaign, but even as she readied the declaration, she realized from the pleased looks on her employers' faces that she was not being given a choice. Or even an opportunity to voice her objections. Dread and anger tangled into a knot in her stomach. She forced a calm expression and a bright smile, but couldn't quell the telltale tremble in her hand as she reached for the nearest photos. "May I see?"

Her heart thudded against her ribs as Quint turned all the photo sheets toward her. Despite BiBi's warning of what to expect, Jane couldn't believe it. The Devil had totally ignored her request and made her the centerpiece of his proposal. Torture by hellfire would be too good for him.

Fury blurred her vision. When it cleared, she was still seeing the same appalling thing. She groaned inwardly. *Dear God, my cheeks are red balloons. My body looks like gigantic mounds of dough. The camera doesn't add ten pounds. It adds twenty.* She wanted to melt, turn liquid, and flow out of the room through the drain in the concrete floor. Nick Taziano was a dead man walking.

"What do you think, Jane? Aren't they fabulous?" Callee enthused with a twinkle in her green eyes.

Jane thought she might throw up. Callee had championed her since the day they met, and she couldn't think of any reason why she would lie to her now. But she was. Jane had eyes; she saw every flaw, every awful thing she had always hated about the way she looked. She blurted out, "I don't photograph well."

"Oh, my God, yes, you do," Callee said. "You're every bit as photogenic as your wonderful pies."

"And these photos make your pies look good enough to eat off the page," Quint said, bringing giggles from the women for his accidental innuendo.

"You're just shy," Andrea said. "But you shouldn't be. This is a great campaign Nick has created."

Only BiBi remained silent, a phony smile on her purple lip-glossed mouth.

Callee nodded her head, her chestnut curls bouncing. "And I love 'Meet the Angel Who Creates Big Sky Pie's Heavenly Desserts.'"

Really? She didn't think that was a bit cornball? Jane's plastered-on smile faltered, but she nodded as if to agree, all the while dying inside. She didn't want these photos on the Internet, where people would see them and smirk about the weight she'd gained, calling her fat behind her back, or worse. She'd suffered enough of that when she'd gone from being a scrawny little kid to a weight-challenged teenager. She thought she'd put the bullying behind her, but the old feelings of self-consciousness pounced like a mugger in an alley.

She slipped onto a stool and went very quiet, as she'd done all through high school, trying to make herself invisible despite knowing that she could not create such an illusion. Her sleight-of-hand skills were limited to the conjuring of exquisite pie. A tear threatened. The Devil had done this to her, stirred up every self-doubt she thought she'd overcome. Was it any wonder she hated him so much? He was going to be very sorry.

Callee said something about the official grand opening, drawing Jane's attention. She shook off her dark thoughts and listened.

"I don't think it will come as any surprise, but in the few weeks since we opened our doors, business has been slowly, steadily increasing," Callee said. "You are all doing great work and should be proud of yourselves. The official grand opening is just three weeks away. We have all kinds of ideas we're playing with to make it an unforgettable success. Free giveaways, special coupons, and if any of you have some ideas, please feel free to share them. BiBi, we'd like you to handle coordinating the pie-eating contest."

BiBi let out a squeak of delight as though she'd been handed the keys and deed to the pie shop. "Oh, thank you."

Jane wondered if her assistant realized how much more work than fun this would involve. Or did BiBi consider this another notch in her belt, something that would help her score points with her dad? If so, that was just sad. Jane said a silent prayer of gratitude for her own father's unconditional love, a love she vowed not ever to take for granted.

The meeting broke up. BiBi gathered her belongings and left. Andrea and Quint went into the café, but Callee had asked Jane to stay for a few minutes. Jane figured that her boss was going to bring up her reaction to the website presentation. This would be her one chance to express her contrary feelings about it before they gave the Devil the go-ahead.

She rehearsed in her head what she wanted to say, but Callee jumped right in gushing over how much she loved the ad proposal and how beautiful Jane was in all of the photos, silencing any protest as easily as Jane trimmed excess dough from a crust.

And then Callee grew serious. "I wanted you to know that Nick told Quint about your childhood history, including that you weren't exactly one big happy family."

Jane curbed the urge to tell her employer it was the worst year of her young life, that Nick had done everything possible to make the situation a hell on earth. She needed to keep in mind that Nick was one of Quint's best friends and expressing her urge to poison his coffee probably wasn't a great idea. "Merging families can be..." Impossible. "Difficult."

Chestnut curls bobbed as Callee nodded in commiseration. "I've heard that. I wouldn't know. I never knew my dad, and my mom died when I was very young. My grandmother raised me." The flash of pain that passed through her usually compassionate eyes told Jane that that had not been a loving relationship, but Callee didn't expand on it. "At any rate, I hope working with Nick isn't going to be uncomfortable for you..."

There. She'd opened the door. All Jane had to do was cross the threshold, tell her how she felt. Tell her now. But she couldn't. Her complaints sounded too whiny, too juvenile—even inside her head. She could only imagine how juvenile they would sound out loud. She heard herself say, "No, it's fine. That was a long time ago. We're past it."

"Really?" Callee seemed relieved, if not totally convinced. "Quint got the impression that Nick was very unhappy about your parents' remarrying."

He'd told Quint? Jane blinked. Of course he had. Best friends did stuff like telling each other their problems.

Jane grappled for composure. She despised sharing anything with Nick, even their mutual disdain for the upcoming reunion of their parents, but she wasn't going to open up to her employer about it. "It's not an ideal situation, but this time around, Nick and I don't have to share a home with them."

"As long as you can get along during this ad campaign, I'll be happy." Callee laughed and gathered the papers she'd brought to the staff meeting. "Oh, speaking of weddings, I had two calls today for potential bookings of Big Sky Pie for upcoming wedding receptions."

"Oh, wow, our first events."

"They aren't booked yet, but they are both scheduled for consultations and tastings."

Jane shucked her apron, stowing it in her bag to take home and launder. "I love that people are actually veering away from the tradition of cake for weddings, that they're considering pies instead." She hadn't expected there would be much demand in Kalispell for pies at weddings, birthdays, or anniversaries, since folks walked pretty traditional lines here, but she hadn't taken into consideration that not everyone liked cake.

"We're becoming popular," Callee said. "Let's hope the trend keeps up, even if it means occasionally taking on extra kitchen staff."

"Quint?" Jane asked, smiling at the possibility. Callee's husband could bake pies that rivaled his mother's and Jane's. Although he didn't care to broadcast that to the world yet, he had let the staff in on it.

"He can definitely pitch in, if needed, but I was thinking that maybe Molly might be able to do some of the pies for the events. It will depend on how she's feeling, of course, and whether or not her doctor approves when the time comes."

"Oh, that would be wonderful." Jane had been hired as Molly's replacement when she suffered a heart attack. Jane welcomed the opportunity to get to know her better, but working with her, ah, that would be a dream come true.

Callee held her papers to her chest. "Tomorrow, right after the lunch rush, one of those bridal couples will be coming in. I'd like you to put together a sampling of the day's pies and then be available to answer any questions they may have. Keep a crisp clean chef coat and hat for that meeting, if you have a spare. Best foot forward, as they say…"

"Were either of the calls you took from a Ms. Scott?" Jane asked, having had an awful thought that perhaps one of the two inquiries could've been from her mother. If the appointment was under *Taziano*, Callee would have said, but Jane's mother might have used her maiden name, the name she'd reclaimed when she opened Rebel Scott, Wedding Planner, Inc.

"Scott?" Callee grew thoughtful. "Nope. Why?"

"If you should receive such a call from Rebel Scott, I'd appreciate a heads-up."

"Your mother?"

Jane nodded, and Callee seemed to need no further explanation. Jane was grateful, since she'd decided not to follow Nick's lead and spill her true feelings about her mother's upcoming nuptials. Callee wasn't her friend. She was her boss. Some lines were not meant to be crossed.

But Callee didn't seem to feel the same way. She was studying Jane like a county fair judge choosing which pie would win the blue ribbon, looking for imperfections she'd missed on first inspection. And finding one. "You're no happier about your mother and Nick's father reuniting than Nick is, are you?"

So much for keeping her silence. *Mental note to self: Don't take up poker for a living.*

Her imagination began conjuring up scenarios of how to murder the Devil. Instead of poisoning his coffee, she could bake him a poisonous pie, but that offered no satisfaction. He deserved worse. Those dreaded photos he'd taken would soon be on the Internet. Jane had but one option.

Chapter Five

⌒

Jane wrote the check before she could change her mind, before self-doubts and insecurities rallied, before fully considering the side effects—such as doing this in front of strangers and, worse, doing it in front of people who knew her. Although in a town this size, the local gym had more overweight, out-of-shape customers than prima donna, hard bodies.

The workout room held the usual exercise equipment and continuous mirrored walls that provided a 360-degree reflection of one's every flaw. Jane had chosen a baggy black T-shirt and sweatpants, the exact opposite of what her new personal trainer, Liam McDougal, wore. A former Canadian ski champ, his every muscled ab and glute was encased in the latest skin-hugging workout wear—royal blue bike shorts and a sleeveless T-shirt in a shade of ice blue that rivaled the color of his eyes and complemented his thatch of white-blond hair.

She avoided direct eye contact with the mirrors and concentrated on what Liam was saying, "A little cardio, a little weight resistance to begin with…"

"And then we'll work up to a lot of cardio and a lot of weight resistance?" Jane smiled through clenched teeth, telling herself this was good for her. Healthy. And she intended to stick to it, at least until she dropped twenty pounds. After contemplating several options for Nick's demise, she'd decided it was more productive to do something for herself than to take out her anger and frustrations on the Devil. Besides, punishing him would require spending time with him. She had too much of that coming in her immediate future.

"First, though, we start with warm-ups, eh?" Liam's longish hair flopped forward onto his forehead as he leaned over to straighten the position of her leg. "Like this."

Warm-ups…sort of like preheating an oven. She could relate.

"These leg stretches will prevent shin splints."

Jane nodded, duplicating his movements, proud of herself that she was getting the hang of it. It wasn't nearly as tough as she'd expected, given her daily exercise amounted to going up and down the three flights of stairs to her apartment and hefting a few dozen pies throughout the day. She wished she'd known shin splints were preventable a couple years ago, clearly recalling the pain she'd experienced after deciding to participate in a two-mile hike with some friends. Just walking for a week or two had been excruciating.

"Okay, do this one now." Liam bent his leg so that

the heel of his sneaker touched his tight rear end, then he reached behind, grabbed the toe of the shoe, and pulled toward his butt. Simple enough to follow. Jane mimicked the leg lift, but the heel of her shoe didn't come anywhere near her bottom, and when she reached around for the toe of the sneaker, she had none of Liam's ease or smoothness.

Good thing she wasn't wearing pink or she'd look like a chubby flamingo, she thought, just as she lost her balance and felt herself toppling. Firm hands grasped her upper arms from behind, rescuing her before she slammed into Liam.

"Whoa, Pain. If you want to jump the PT's bones, maybe you should do it somewhere less public."

Jane went rigid. Nick. Where in hell had he come from? She jerked free of his grip, forgetting to release her hand from her foot first, and instantly tipped over. This time both men grabbed for her, missed, and her knees slammed into the concrete floor. Screaming pain radiated from the point of impact outward, while steam heat flared in her toes and raced to her scalp. She didn't need to check one of the gazillion mirrors to know how crimson her face was. Bing cherry red. She waved the men off, cringing in agony, holding back tears. It actually hurt too much to cry.

Exercisers leaped from stationary bikes, treadmills, and elliptical trainers and came running to gape at their fallen comrade, their faces full of shock and curiosity and pity. *Why did the whole world seem to be watching her lately, judging her, finding fault?*

"Everybody step back. Please. She's fine," Nick said, and surprisingly the mini-crowd dispersed, mumbling to one another. Probably about what a klutz she was.

Liam and Nick seemed to be squaring off, each about to claim her as *his* damsel in distress. Jane blushed. She'd always envisioned the "every girl's fantasy of two men fighting over her" as romantic, not as a most embarrassing moment. Liam blinked first, ending the awkward man-dance with Nick, offering to go fetch a painkiller and a couple of ice packs, leaving Nick to help her into a sitting position.

As he departed, Nick squatted beside her, his gaze following Liam, his words for her ears only. "He's worried you'll sue the gym."

She made a face. "Always so quick to judge everyone, aren't you?"

He showed no reaction to the gibe, his expression as warm as a winter breeze, but his hands were quick and gentle as he pushed her sweatpants up above her knees. Without asking first. "There's no blood, nothing scraped, but both caps are scarlet and already showing patches of bruising."

She could tell Nick was trying not to hurt her, using only slight pressure, but she winced once or twice when his fingers connected with the injured areas. He said, "I don't think anything is broken. There's some swelling, but it's minor. The worst that could happen is maybe some water on the knee."

"You're making that up." What did he know about injuries like this? Nothing. He was an adman, not a doctor. "There is no such thing as water on the knee...is there?"

He smirked, shaking his head. "Your education is sorely lacking, Pain. A couple of years ago, I slipped in the bathroom. Wet floor. Knee slammed the bathtub so hard I almost passed out. Doc said it was the same injury as if that area had hit the dashboard in a car wreck. It was sore and stiff right away, but the pain seemed to leave quickly while the stiffness got minimally worse each day. On day four, I suddenly couldn't bend my knee, couldn't climb the stairs. The area around the knee was the size of a football. If that happens, they have to suck out the fluid with a long needle. Sounds worse than it is. The knee was so swollen, I couldn't feel the needle. I swear."

Concern swept over Jane. "My knees feel hot. Is that a bad symptom?"

"Want me to run you to the ER?"

"No." She didn't want him driving her anywhere. Liam maybe. But not Nick. "Please, just go away."

Nick glanced around, spotting a few curious onlookers still lingering nearby. "Maybe the gawkers will go away if you get up off the floor and show them you're not critical."

He reached out to help her up. She shooed him off. "I can do it on my own."

But she couldn't. She stopped fussing and took his hand, noticing for the first time that he also wore black, long, loose-fitting shorts and an oversized tank, a white towel around his neck. His every asset wasn't on display like Liam's, and perversely, she found that intriguing.

He lifted her with the ease it would take to hoist a kitten. "You should elevate those legs as well as ice them and do it as soon as possible. I live right around the corner—"

"Liam's bringing ice, and then I'll go straight home—where I also have ice," Jane said, her gaze flicking to his defined arms. Just how defined was he under that shirt? Under those shapeless shorts? And why did she care? What was wrong with her? He couldn't help being sexy, but she didn't have to notice and...and fantasize about him. She needed to get out of here. Get away from Nick. This was all his fault. If he hadn't kissed her, if she hadn't enjoyed his kisses, she wouldn't be wondering what else he could make her feel. If he hadn't taken those photos that exposed how awful she looked, how out of shape she was, she wouldn't have signed up for the gym. Wouldn't now have black-and-blue knees.

She should have stuck with her first plan and baked him a poisonous pie.

"Thanks. I can take it from here." But as she began to walk, the hurt intensified. Liam arrived with Tylenol and a bottle of water. But no ice. "Sorry, someone forgot to put the gel packs back into the freezer."

"That's okay. I'll just go home." She swallowed the pills, then held the water bottle to the worst injury. The cold did ease the stinging.

"Come on," Nick caught her shoulders. "I'll walk you to your car."

"I can do that," Liam said, stepping to her other side.

She shrugged off Nick and took Liam's arm, but halfway to the door, she pulled up short. "Oh, wait, my gym bag. It's in the ladies' locker room."

She gave Liam the key. He sent one of the female employees to retrieve it, and three minutes later, they were outside going to the car. Moving with the speed of a snail, Jane leaned on Liam. Nick trailed behind, carrying her bag, acting as though he didn't trust Liam to walk a woman to her car. She unlocked the Jeep and instantly realized it was too tall for her to climb into, given the aching and tightness in her knees.

"I'll lift you in," Nick volunteered.

"Yeah, me too," Liam said.

Summer shoppers traversed the sidewalk, casting sidelong glances at her handsome escorts. If they were looking at her now, imagine what they'd do if the two guys attempted to heft her into the Jeep. No thanks. No more negative attention. "I can do this."

She could, damn it. She grabbed the steering wheel and pulled, but hoisting one stiff leg or the other higher than the frame was impossible. Her pecs needed serious work. *Note to self: Add weight lifting to my gym routine.* The second Nick reached for her bottom to boost her up, she cried out, slapped at his hands, and gave up. She stood by the vehicle, frustration radiating off her like the shimmers of heat off the pavement.

"I've got it from here, McDougal," Nick said. "Shouldn't you be getting back to work?"

Liam glanced at the gym, then at Jane, and gave an apologetic shrug. "Give me a call when you're ready for your next session. I'll make sure it's not so brutal."

Jane thanked him, then braced herself for Nick to lift her into the Jeep, but he was shaking his head. "If you can't climb in, you can't drive. Your gas and brake pedal reactions would be too slow."

He had a point. Stubbornly refusing his help was what Grandma Wilson would call biting off her nose to save her face. "All right, then drive me home."

"My place is closer, and there are no stairs."

She'd forgotten about the three flights to her apartment. She sighed and relinquished the Jeep keys. "Just because I'm letting you help me does not mean we're friends."

Nick nodded, but his dimples betrayed a smile. "Yeah, I got that memo. In bold print. I'm nothing more to you than a Good Samaritan." He relocked the Jeep, grasped hold of her arm, and taking small, slow steps, guided her down the street another block and a half to a store door wedged between two shops. Lettering on the glass identified it as the location of Adz R Taz. "I live and work upstairs."

"Stairs," Jane squeaked when he let them into the building. "You said no stairs."

He answered by sweeping her into his arms, startling her, and making her self-conscious all over again. "No, Nick, please don't, I—I—I'm too heavy..." There, she'd said it.

His dark brows rose, and he pulled her tighter to his hard chest, his eyes narrowed as though he were pissed off. "Don't say things like that about yourself."

His response so surprised her that she stopped struggling to be released. She put her arms around his neck, locking her hands at his nape, fearful he'd discover she was more than he could handle and that they'd tumble down the steps before he could reach the landing. He didn't go up the stairs, however, but strode down the hall, stopping at another door.

"Private elevator," Nick said. "My customers come in all ages and disabilities."

She just bet they did. "In that case, you can put me down. I can still stand, remember?"

"That's okay." He continued cradling her in his arms, which had, she realized, eased the pressure somewhat on her knees. He moved into the small space and punched the second-floor button. "I don't mind."

"Maybe I mind," she said, loosening her grip on his neck, catching a nose full of key lime scent.

His smoldering gaze seemed to hold her, like invisible hands cupping her face. "Really, Pain, don't you like it when a man holds you like this?"

And then he was staring at her mouth with a hunger that released a sensuous sigh deep within her. A breath shuddered out. Think of something else. Anything but those bone-melting kisses. "D-Do you own this building?"

"Changing the subject won't make me want to kiss you less."

"No more kissing."

"Are you sure?" He lowered his mouth to hers, heating that sensitive flesh with a soft breath, and a lustful tremor ran through her.

She couldn't lie. She wanted another kiss, and so much more. Who could blame her? Those chocolate eyes, those sinful dimples. She felt light-headed. "I'm sure."

"Well, then, if you're sure." The elevator came to a stop, and the door slid open on a large landing. "The McCoys own this building. I lease this upper floor. It's an open loft with a bedroom, bath, and kitchenette. I do a lot of my work online, and it's easier for me to set my own hours, work all night and sleep all day if I choose. Plus, I'm on the road so much that low maintenance suits my purposes."

As they exited the elevator, she spied the stairwell to their left. Nick carried her in the opposite direction to a huge steel door. A moment later, they crossed the threshold bride and groom style. Only this was no honeymoon. This was the Devil carrying her into his lair as if she had no will to resist. She wasn't hurting that badly.

She struggled to get him to release her, but he took her to one of two easy chairs angled toward a humongous, wall-mounted, flat-screen TV, setting her down as though she were precious cargo, propping her legs gently on a leather ottoman. The other end of this basketball-court space seemed to be his work area.

Light poured in through factory-sized windows mounted in distressed brick walls and highlighted several giant, framed photos that were hung throughout as though in an art gallery. There were pictures depicting a variety of subjects, some inanimate objects, some real-life events, and some posed, studio models. The compelling prints dared you to look away. She couldn't. Each one was more intriguing than the last.

Nick headed to a wall that served as his kitchenette and pulled open the freezer compartment on his fridge. He returned to her side, spread a thin dish towel on each knee, and then the frozen gel packs.

She winced at the sudden, intense chill. "I don't suppose you've got anything to drink besides water?"

"Whiskey?"

She shook her head. Though a shot or two might relieve the dull ache of her wounds, she didn't need her resistance to Nick lowered even a notch.

"Beer?" he said.

She wrinkled her nose. She was not a beer drinker. "Coffee?"

"That I can do."

She laid her head back against the leather chair and shut her eyes, willing the Tylenol to kick in. She had no idea she'd drifted to sleep, or how long she slept, probably only a few minutes, but when she awoke, the smell of coffee was strong and appealing.

Nick stood at the counter, filling two mugs. "How do you like yours?"

"With fake sugar."

"Don't have any. You want the real thing?"

"No, that's okay." She already ingested too much sugar on a daily basis when taste-testing the pie fillings, and if she hoped to lose weight, sugar intake had to be restricted whenever possible. "Do you have any cream?"

"Milk." He smiled. "It's two percent."

"Do you still drink milk straight from the container?" Although that was a typical male thing to do, she hoped he knew it was also about the most revolting thing women could imagine.

He crooked his head and shrugged, a smirk displaying the dimples. "I live alone. What can I say?"

She rolled her eyes, disgusted, not bothering to hide how she felt. "I'll do without then."

"Suit yourself," he said, though his eyes seemed to be asking if she was always so hard to please. He brought the coffee to her and sat on the edge of the ottoman. "You're one of those high-maintenance dates, aren't you?"

"I beg your pardon?" She nearly spewed coffee at him. "Are you comparing this to...to a date?"

"God no. It was just an expression. Never mind." But he was shaking his head, a smile in his eyes as he sipped his coffee. "Are you feeling any better? Worse?"

"About the same, but the ice does feel good." No sense biting his head off. He was trying. Really trying. Plus, this was one of the best cups of coffee that she'd had in years. She wondered what his secret was, but doubted he'd tell her if she asked. She didn't ask. She would finish her coffee and leave.

He lifted one of the ice packs and turned it over. "How long have you been a member of the gym?"

About two and a half hours, Jane thought, glancing toward his wall clock. But he didn't need to know that...or any of her other personal business. She said, "A while now."

"It's kind of strange that we haven't bumped into each other there before today."

Yeah, imagine. If she'd known he belonged to the gym, she wouldn't have been so quick to write that check today. Before she could suggest they were there at different times due to their personal schedules, his phone sounded the arrival of a text or e-mail. He glanced at the screen. His eyes grew dark, and when he set the phone down, he switched the subject so fast it almost gave Jane whiplash.

"Regarding our parents," he said, broaching the subject that had been like an elephant in the room. He sank onto the arm of the chair, his citrus scent surrounding her. "I spent half the morning e-mailing and phoning my dad's closest friends, trying to find out what caused the divorce fifteen years ago. That text was from one of his best pals."

"And?" Jane lifted her gaze to his, eager for the results.

"And so far, nothing. A big fat zero. How about you? Women like to gossip more than men. Surely someone was forthcoming with you."

Women were worse gossips than men? Not in her experience. She just shook her head at his idiocy. At least he'd made an effort. It was her idea to contact their parents' friends, but she hadn't made one call yet today. Guilt spiraled through her. But before she could admit it, a doorbell sounded.

"Someone downstairs," Nick said, scrambling up and over to an intercom. He asked who it was, and the response sent a chill through Jane.

"It's your old man, Nicky. Let me in, son."

Her eyes wide, she hopped off the chair so fast that dish towels and gel packs dropped to the floor. She grabbed her bag and headed for the door. "Thanks for the ice and coffee. I'm moving well enough to drive now."

"Are you sure?"

She wasn't, but it didn't matter. She grabbed her bag and walked to the door as fast as possible. "I'm not sticking around to chat with your father."

"There's no back way out." Nick held the door as she slipped into the hallway and spoke softly. "But Dad always comes up in the elevator. Do you think you can manage the stairs?"

"Absolutely." She was walking better. Her knees were flexible again. That had to mean there wasn't any swelling to speak of. The ice had definitely done the trick. She had almost reached the top of the stairs when she heard footsteps ascending, a man whistling. She did a rapid retreat, found the door to the elevator still open on the second floor, and slipped inside, pressing herself to an inside wall. Her heart thudded so loudly she was sure it was rattling the small cage.

Romeo Taziano came into view a second later, dressed in summer golf attire, tan slacks, striped polo shirt, and beige loafers. She could see why her mother was attracted to him, given his silver-streaked hair, his bold features, his sense of style, and that quick smile. A real heartbreaker. The thought gave her pause. Had Romeo cheated on her mother? Was that the reason the marriage had ended? *Once a heartbreaker, always a heartbreaker.*

She liked the possibility. It explained why her mother always felt the need to be loved. And if it were true, Jane had real ammunition to convince her mom to reconsider this latest marriage.

Jane pressed against the elevator wall so neither man would see her, as Nick stepped into the hallway and said, "Hey, old man, how's it hanging?"

"A little less low these days."

Male laugher reverberated through the hallway.

Jane peeked out. Father and son were embracing, a male hug with shoulder slapping and big grins. They were obviously very close. As Nick shoved the door inward and gestured his father into the loft, Romeo said, "Rebel is fretting her pretty head off, son. We need to know how your plan to win Jane over to our side is working out."

Chapter Six

❧

Bending and straightening, two simple movements that Jane took for granted, tortured her the next day. So much so that she assigned several jobs to BiBi that she would normally do herself. At their lunch break, Andrea inspected her knees and cooed sympathetically over the bruising and slight swelling. Jane said, "Do your little boys realize how lucky they are to have such a great mom?"

"I'm the lucky one." Andrea beamed, the love she felt for her children alight in her eyes. "They make it easy on me."

"I can't wait to meet them."

"Oh, you will. You know what, I have some Asper-creme in my purse. I'll bet it would ease some of that residual pain you're dealing with."

"I'll try anything at this point." The salve was cool, a bit sticky, but didn't smell bad, and it seemed to work quickly. If only a salve could soothe the anger that curled in her belly like a mean little ball. She wasn't even sure all of it was directed at Nick. She knew better than to trust him. He was a devil at thirteen; he was a devil still. His disarming charm belonged to a trickster, and she'd been truly tricked. She'd let her guard down, falling for his heroic actions after her mishap at the gym, believing his earnest plea to help break off the engagement. Fool. Stupid, stupid fool. And yet, she could not shake that man out of her head, could not let go of the desire to explore more than a few kisses with him.

She took a bottle of ice-cold water out to the back stoop, settling down on one of the wrought iron patio chairs placed there for the employees to use during breaks. A moment later, Andrea joined her.

"I think I'm losing my mind," Jane said, not meaning to voice this out loud.

Andrea glanced up from the e-book she'd been reading. "Man trouble?"

"How'd you guess?" Jane couldn't believe that she was so transparent. Or was it that Andrea was older, a bit more experienced, a lot wiser?

"I don't know. Something in your eyes." Andrea pushed her thick blond hair behind her ear, her expression one Jane imagined she might offer a younger sister. "What's going on?"

"Well, there's this guy, and we've kissed a few times," Jane said, hesitating, uncertain of the wisdom of being so forthcoming with one of her bosses, but the need to unburden herself overrode everything. "I don't want a relationship with this guy, or any guy. It's not like I'm looking to get engaged or married. Not right now. Maybe never. I want to keep my focus on my career, but..."

Andrea was nodding. "But you're young and healthy and have needs, and for some reason that only the love gods know, this guy is ringing all your whistles and bells?"

Jane exhaled, nodding, relieved she hadn't had to spell it out. "Yeah, that."

Andrea leaned in and lowered her voice conspiratori- ally, as though someone lurking in the back alley might overhear. "In my experience, if you want a guy out of your head, get him into your bed. That usually sates the lust and curbs that dangerous, seductive curiosity."

The suggestion sent a blush over Jane's skin, and she knew she was pink as a grapefruit. She was so not the girl who manipulated a guy into bed. She wouldn't even know how to start. And even if she was guilty of some dangerous, seductive curiosity where Nick was concerned, she would no more act on that now than eat rocks. Not after finding out his kisses had ulterior mo- tives. "Perhaps that would have been a good idea, but there's been an unexpected twist in the mix. I just found out his so-called interest has a nefarious bent."

"Whoa. That puts a whole new spin on things. I'm sorry, by the way. Men are such dogs." Andrea's face was a mix of sympathy and disgust. She'd obviously had similar experiences. "Does he know that you know?"

"No."

A gleam of mischief danced in Andrea's eyes. "Good. Then here's what you do..."

The rest of the day passed quickly, the routine and chattering of her coworkers allowing Jane the opportunity to dwell on Andrea's suggestion to give Nick a dose of his own medicine, and to imagine a few dozen scenarios of how she would do just that. The mental exercise produced so many sexy thoughts of Nick that she'd wanted to vent her frustration and anger on the dough. She resisted that urge. Beating up the dough would not give her the release or satisfaction she sought, only make tomorrow's baking a challenge she didn't need.

Nick was going to be sorry he'd messed with her. Very sorry. She stored the last of the dough mounds for the next day in the Sub-Zero, leaving the cleanup to her assistant and retrieving her bag. In her Jeep, she took the time to check her phone. There were several missed calls from her mother and a couple of texts. *Can't avoid Mom forever.* She made the call and a date to meet for drinks.

And an hour later, she was seated at a table in the bar of MacKenzie River Pizza Company with a glass of chardonnay to steady her nerves. She'd suggested this restaurant for its high-backed, private booths. Mom would never bawl her out in public, but in case the discussion became too revealing, it offered a level of privacy.

Her mother came in wearing floral crop pants and a gauzy yellow top that gave her lithe body the look of a model on a runway. As Rebel made her way to the table on wedged espadrilles, her long brown hair swinging against her shoulders, Jane noticed the heads of men and women alike turning to glance after her, but Rebel Scott seemed oblivious to the attention she drew; she only had eyes for Jane.

Jane's nerves jumped, and she reached for her wine. She'd had a whole speech worked out before the engagement party the other night, before she'd even known who her mother intended to marry, but by choosing to run out, Jane knew she'd leveled the playing field and given her mother reason to be upset with her. She mentally ticked off possible grievances: bad manners, embarrassing Mom in front of friends, avoiding her phone calls and texts.

Yeah, but I was blindsided.

And from the hint of contrition in her mother's amber eyes, Mom seemed to own that. As Jane realized this, she wondered why families had to be so complicated. Why expectations seemed always too high to meet. She wiped her palms on the skirt of her ankle-length, baby pink sundress, and stood up to greet her mother with a hug.

The hug was awkward. Jane had put off contacting her mom too long; punishment for that misdeed was to be expected. And there was also the tension of neither knowing how to approach the one thing they both wished to discuss.

Rebel sat and ordered a margarita. "Smells wonderful in here. I haven't had pizza in ages."

Probably for years, Jane thought, since her mother

embraced the L.A. mentality when it came to food. Thin is better than . . . fill in the blank. "They don't offer only pizza. There are salads, sandwiches, et cetera, if you're hungry."

"Well, I'm not really. Are you?"

"Why don't we share an appetizer then?"

They ordered stuffed mushrooms, and a wall of silence ensued. Jane watched her mother play with her engagement ring, a double-digit-carat diamond from the size of it. A memory came of the ring Romeo had given Mom fifteen years ago, the diamond so small it required a magnifying glass to see. Nick's dad was a mechanic back then, a one-man operation, making barely enough each week to keep the rent paid, while Mom worked nights bartending, her salary spent on food and utilities. He must have struck gold in Vegas.

But then Mom's business was also doing well. Very well. Jane broke the silence. "Do you have a pre-nup?"

Her mother's gaze lifted, and she laughed that tinkling, pure-bell tone, catching the attention of the other bar patrons. "Darling, this isn't my first dance at the ball."

My mother, the queen of understatement. But she couldn't have given Jane a better opening. "And that's the heart of my concern, Mom. What are you doing? Haven't you realized after six previous marriages that getting married isn't the solution to whatever it is that keeps driving you down the aisle?"

"Can't you just be happy for Romeo and me?"

Jane blanched. Oh, how she wished she could answer

a resounding "Yes" to that question, but she couldn't. At times like this, she felt like the mother and her mother was like the child. Mom needed saving...from herself. Jane had only her best interests at heart. "Do you remember my fifteenth birthday?"

"Vividly. That's the day you told me you wanted no part of Rebel Scott Wedding Planner, Inc."

"That's the day I told you my heart's desire was to be a pastry chef. And do you recall what you told me? Because I've never forgotten it."

Mom's brows knit, and she gave a slight shake of her head. "I hope it was good advice?"

The best. "You said if that was what I wanted to do with my life, then I should always remember to keep my eye on the prize, not let anything deter me from that path. That there would be boys and men along the way who would try to tempt me, but that I should never mistake lust for love. That if I decided to stop and enjoy what they offered, to have fun, but to always protect myself, to make sure I called the shots, and that I could walk away and keep on toward the future that I had mapped out for myself. I've lived by that advice, Mom."

Rebel smiled. "You've done what you set out to do, and I'm very proud of you, Jane."

Jane wasn't fishing for compliments. She wanted to ask her mother how she could give such great advice, but couldn't take it? Somehow the words stuck on her tongue, so she put it as delicately as she could. "You taught me that I don't need a man to complete me. It was wonderful advice, something every young woman should hear and heed."

"Yes, well, I didn't have a mother as wise as yours," she said on a strained laugh, obviously seeking to bring a lighter tone back to the conversation.

A sip of chardonnay offered a moment's reprieve for Jane to gather her thoughts. She was not making the point she meant to make. Maybe a straightforward attack would be best. "Why would you remarry someone who broke your heart as badly as Romeo did fifteen years ago? I don't get it."

Her mother set the margarita glass on the table, and a light—as golden as the tequila in her drink—entered her eyes. "I never got over him."

The little girl inside Jane didn't want to hear that someone other than her daddy might have been the love of her mother's life. But the grown-up Jane feared it might be true, that this was likely the most honest her mother had been in many years. With Jane, and with herself. The mushrooms arrived. Jane transferred one to her plate, but didn't eat. "Why did you two break up the first time?"

Rebel touched the salt on the rim of her glass, then sucked it from her finger. "Oh, you know, the usual. We were young..."

"You were twenty-eight."

"We weren't financially mature. Though we both worked hard, the budget never seemed to meet our requirements. We began to fight about money..."

Had they? Jane didn't recall any fights about money

or any extravagant purchases. More like "no, we can't afford that" whenever she or the Devil asked for something. "And now that you're both financially secure, you don't think you'll fight about money?"

"Like you said, 'pre-nup.'"

"What's yours is yours and what's his is his. How very sane and logical of you." As if her mother had ever gone into any of her marriages doing the sane and logical thing. This was bogus, but Jane didn't know why.

Rebel smiled. "So, my darling, now that your doubts are laid to rest, please say you'll be my maid of honor."

What? This was a first. One of her many girlfriends had always had that role. She could see how important this was to Mom, that she'd hoped Jane would be pleased to be asked and would immediately accept. Jane was pleased, but her doubts were not dead and buried. They loomed bigger than ever. "I—I can't..." Her mother's expression fell, and Jane could see the hurt she was causing, so she added, "...give you an answer just now. I need a little more time. Please try to understand."

"Of course, sweetheart. You don't need to decide this minute." But her mother's chin came up as if to ward off a direct hit to the heart. "Nick is going to be Romeo's best man."

"He is?" Jane tried, but failed, to hide her surprise.

"He and his father are very close." Rebel stabbed at a mushroom, then glanced at Jane with those clear golden eyes that now seemed like sautéed butter sizzling at the edges. "In fact, I thought you'd be more receptive to my offer... since Nick told his dad you were coming around about the wedding."

"I see." So Nick was lying to everyone. Why was that surprising? *What could you expect from a devil?* It was time this devil paid his due. "Remember how I used to feel about Nick?"

Her mother made a face. "Oh, dear."

"Exactly. I wouldn't put much stock in anything he says about me. We are not friends." Or allies. Or anything else. Nick just didn't know it yet.

Jane hugged her mother good-bye and promised to give her an answer in a day or two, then she drove home, the ten-minute drive allowing plenty of time to mull over the puzzling aspects of their conversation. Why had Mom lied about money ending the marriage to Nick's dad? What had really driven her mother and Romeo to divorce?

All she'd concluded by the time she'd reached her apartment was that she needed a lot more information than she had. But where to get it? Who might know? She considered that question during a warm bath for her still tender knees, and as she was toweling off, it came to her.

She dressed, wrangled a dinner invite, and a half an hour later, she was driving past Wilson's Auto Barn, home of GMC, Jeep, and Dodge on I-93, and a mile farther on, turning down the side road that led to the private residence her dad and stepmom had built twelve years ago. One of the blueberry pies she'd made today rode on the passenger seat. The house where Jane had spent most of her teenage years came into view, a sprawling rambler with a full basement, set on a rise in the center of ten acres. Woods served as a natural fence, and the creek that ran through the backyard could be seen from the window of the large, farmhouse kitchen.

She arrived early with purpose. She needed to talk to her grandmother. Though Wilma Wilson lived with her son and his second wife, she had her own mother-in-law suite with a kitchen built with pie baking in mind. She'd taught Jane to create the perfect buttery crust long before food processors came into being. Long before Jane could reach the counter without standing on the kitchen stool.

Jane found her seated on her padded rocker, waiting with a cup of tea and a sympathetic ear. At seventy, Gram remained a force with which to reckon, though one might not guess it from her soft exterior: puffy white hair, puffy body, a smile that could bring on a sugar high.

Wilma loved nothing as much as a good gossip session, and her disarming appearance brought out the need to unburden their secrets in most everyone who crossed her path. She didn't even wait for Jane to open the conversation. "I hoped you were bringing me the scoop on the engagement and upcoming wedding, but from the look on your pretty face, I'm guessing that's not the case. Sit down, sweetheart, and tell your Gram what has you looking like you've lost your best friend."

Hoping she didn't look as bad as all that, Jane took the love seat near the rocker, skipping the sugar and adding cream to her tea. "Gram, I thought maybe you could tell me something about Mom and Dad's divorce."

"Well, now what got you thinking about that?" A wary glint flickered in her grandmother's eyes, and she fidgeted with the doily on the armrest, a sure sign the subject made her uncomfortable.

"I was just wondering," Jane said, "what role her current fiancé played in the split?"

The rocking chair stopped rocking, and Wilma's nose wrinkled as if her tea were suddenly sour, but she kept her voice soft, a little too sweet. "I'm not sure that it's such a good idea to stir up old ashes."

The response surprised Jane. In the past, her grandmother had had plenty to say on the subject of her mother, most of it unfit for a daughter to hear, and Jane knew, if she could get her to let down her guard, she might learn what she wanted to know. "If those old ashes are as cold as you say, then why not stir them up and blow them away?"

Wilma looked as if Jane had just released her from a cage. "The wisdom of children, they say...I'll admit I'm not one bit pleased that Rebel decided to come back here to marry that, that"—she cleared her throat— "Italian. Why not do the deed in Vegas? I'll tell you why. She wanted to rub my Eddie's nose in it. Love of his life, she was. Love. Of. His. Life. He never recovered from her betrayal. Never."

Jane had heard this tirade before over the years, but never with such venom. She glanced around sharply, glad to discover they were still alone, and wondering how thick the walls were. She didn't want her stepmom hearing this vitriol and being hurt by the hateful words. Vicky might not be perfect, but she loved Jane's dad, and she'd been very good to Wilma over the years.

Deciding it was time to reel Gram in a bit, she asked, "Are you saying that Romeo is the reason Mom and Dad broke up?"

"That's not a question for me."

Seriously? Jane's frustration stuck in her throat. She had a sudden empathy for gerbils running around those little wheels and getting nowhere fast. "Can't you tell me something, Gram?"

Wilma looked over the rim of her half-glasses. "I don't want to hurt you, child, but the fact is, Rebel always thought she was too good for my Eddie. Beauty pageant mentality. A contestant, that's all she was. A wannabe."

Jane's cup landed awkwardly on its saucer, the ensuing clink sounding as though it might have cracked. A wannabe? Was Gram drinking straight Earl Grey or had she laced it with the brandy she kept secreted at the back of the cupboard? The bottle she thought no one knew about. "Gram, my mother was Miss Montana."

Wilma's aqua eyes, so like Jane's, widened as though she'd let something slip she shouldn't have. Or had Jane imagined that? Wilma made a quick recovery, waving her "moment" away with her hand as though it hadn't happened. "Oh, sure, well, I know that. I'm not senile, you know. It's just she fell victim to the lure of prize money and fame, fed to her by those newspaper reporters and contest judges. Rebel got a swelled head, an inflated idea that she was something more special than she was. Or is."

Jane started to get angry. She could say whatever she wanted about her mother. And sometimes did. But she would tolerate only so much of Wilma's bitterness. There was a line not to cross, and Gram had just put her foot on that line. "Enough."

Wilma stopped the easy motion of her rocker and reached to touch Jane's arm. "Oh, my, I'm sorry, sweetheart. I just get riled up too quick. I shouldn't speak like that to you about your mother. Please tell your Gram that you forgive her…"

Jane could never stay mad at Gram, no matter what. She nodded, smiled, and willed the subject a fast death, but she had yet to learn anything helpful and had to dig deeper. "Do you know why Mom and Romeo got divorced?"

Jane was eleven when she came back to live with her dad and Vicky, after her mother and the Devil's father split up. She'd stayed with her mother only over the summer months after that. And every other holiday. Usually in California. Her own memories of that time were as self-centered as most preteens. She was just glad Romeo and his son were no longer in her life. She hadn't given much thought as to why her mother always seemed so sad then.

Wilma shrugged, clearly thinking before speaking now. "The Italian probably got tired of her primping ways—same as your daddy did."

Really? Gram didn't have details, some slight clue even to the truth of the matter? Disappointment jabbed Jane. Every time she thought she'd found someone who could fill her in on the past, it led to another dead end. "Could they have broken up over money? Or lack of money?"

Gram was shaking her head. "I don't see how. I recall his auto mechanic business was a going concern. And your mother made good tips every night bartending, I imagine. Not to mention what your daddy paid in child support, medical, and dental for you."

At last, confirmation for something: Money had not been the death knell to Mom and Romeo's marriage.

"Pumpkin!" Her dad's pet name for her resounded in his booming voice as he bustled into his mother's living quarters without knocking. "I saw your Jeep out front. Vicky says you're joining us for supper. Best news I've had in a month of Sundays."

Eddie Wilson was tall and well built, with auburn hair, leathery-tanned skin, and a grin that warmed the hearts of family and friends and loosened the pocketbooks of car-shopping customers throughout the Flathead Valley. Jane abandoned her tea to meet him halfway and be swallowed up in a bear hug. He had the amazing ability to make her feel small yet protected at the same time. And he always smelled of Old Spice.

She snuggled in his arms, recalling so many times when one of his reassuring hugs was all she needed for a boost. He released her. "Vicky says dinner is ready. I hope you two are hungry. Did you bring a pie?"

"Does Eddie Wilson sell more cars than anyone else in Kalispell?" Jane laughed at the old joke, reassuring him that she had definitely brought a pie.

"What kind?" His metabolism allowed him to eat almost constantly and never gain an ounce.

She wished she'd inherited that gene, and supposed since she hadn't that joining the gym was long overdue. "Blueberry."

He placed a hand over his heart and sighed. "Maybe we should eat dessert first tonight."

"Don't let your wife hear that," Gram said, rising.

"Darn it, Mama, you're no fun." He laughed. "Come then, ladies, let's get to the dining room. The pot roast needs slicing."

Vicky set the tossed salad on the table, next to the mashed potatoes and gravy, then took her place across from Eddie. She might never take a blue ribbon for beauty, but she deserved a prize for trying harder. She worked like a fiend to maintain a size two figure, just as she maintained an impeccable, if austere, home. The only warmth in the décor came from cheerily painted walls.

Her personal fashion sense, however, missed the mark; her wardrobe was full of big bold patterns and unflattering hues that clashed with her brassy blond hair, dresses that seemed to swallow her tiny frame. Tonight's choice resembled something straight from Betsey Johnson's retro line, polka dots and tulle. Somehow her "less is more" gene didn't register when she looked in a mirror.

She excelled, however, in the kitchen, her meals uninspired but always good.

No one mentioned the impending wedding or anything to do with her father's auto dealership at dinner. Vicky and Wilma wanted only to discuss Big Sky Pie, Jane's job, the McCoy family, and the upcoming grand opening. Her dad just wanted to enjoy some of her pie—which he did, heated, with a scoop of ice cream.

After dessert, her dad and grandmother cleared the table and retreated to the kitchen to do the dishes. Jane and Vicky remained at the dining room table, sipping iced coffee, a warm breeze drifting through the open patio doors. "We trade off," Vicky explained. "If I cook, they do the dishes. If Wilma cooks, I do the dishes."

"Sounds fair." Jane sipped her cold drink, wishing she felt closer to her stepmom than she did. She'd tolerated Vicky as one did a houseguest who'd overstayed their welcome, an interloper who'd be leaving as soon as her parents reconciled. Typical thinking for a kid of divorce. Jane realized, now that she was an adult, how unfair she'd been to Vicky and wished she knew a way to defuse the hostility Vicky exhibited toward her whenever they were alone.

Jane found it best to keep all conversations with her stepmom neutral and as upbeat as possible, even if she felt exhausted at the end of them. Tonight, however, she'd run out of things to say about the pie shop's grand opening so she said, "Looks like you've been busy in the garden. The flowers are gorgeous out front."

Vicky was staring at her painted fingernails as if the

swirly pattern that adorned them held a coded message, her expression sullen. "Jane, I overheard your conversation with Wilma earlier."

The words resounded like a dropped platter. *Oh shit.* Jane's cheeks heated. She could only imagine how much her grandmother's words about her mom had stung. "I'm sorry, Vicky. I'm sure Gram didn't mean what she was saying."

Vicky rolled her eyes. "Oh, please. She meant it, every nasty word, but that's okay. I've heard it all before. It quit hurting me years ago."

Jane nodded, squirming in her seat, uncertain if she should or could do anything to erase the hurt Vicky denied, the hurt evident in her gaze. Jane covered her stepmom's hand with her own. "I'm sorry."

Vicky startled at the gesture and pulled back, looking away.

Jane wanted nothing more than to leave. "You know, um, it's getting late, and I should probably go. Three a.m. comes pretty early. I'll just go tell Dad and Gram—"

"You asked her if she knew why Rebel and Romeo broke up."

Jane had started to stand up. She froze, her gaze locking on Vicky's face as she tried reading the cold light in her eyes. "Are you saying that you know the reason?"

She motioned Jane back into her seat, a ghost of a smile appearing on her thin lips. "Not that I could swear to in court, or even on a Bible, but I know when you came to live with us that you were one very unhappy child." She took a swallow of iced coffee, then went on. "The awful stories you told us about Romeo's son. How much he didn't like Rebel. How he was always balking against her authority, telling her that she wasn't his mother, that he didn't have to do anything she said."

Vicky spoke with the sympathy of someone who'd been on the brunt end of exactly this same kind of undeserved treatment, and Jane knew a moment of pure guilt. No doubt she had said exactly the same thing to Vicky. What stepkid hadn't so cruelly addressed a stepparent?

"A miserably unhappy child can harm, and even destroy, an adult relationship," Vicky said, taking another sip of iced coffee. "It causes parents to divide, to choose between their child and their spouse. Most parents will choose their child every time."

Her words stunned Jane. She'd been about to revel in the newfound knowledge that the breakup was the fault of the Devil himself, but flashes of memory were popping in her mind like kernels of corn in sizzling peanut oil. Some of what Vicky had said sounded like things her ten-year-old self had spewed at Romeo. Relentlessly. Never accepting him as a parent. Constantly complaining to her mother. She shoved her drink away as appalling suspicions crept through her. "Are you accusing Nick and me of breaking up that marriage?"

"Oh, God no, sweetie, I'm not accusing anyone of anything." Vicky managed a shocked expression that Jane wasn't buying for a hot minute. "I'm just saying that maybe meshing a family proved more difficult than Romeo and Rebel expected going into their marriage."

The accusation stabbed through Jane like a knife. *I never got over him.* God, were Nick and she at the root of their parents' marriage splitting apart at the seams? The cause of their years of unhappiness? The thought played havoc with her stomach.

"Oh, don't take this to heart, Jane. I'm sure it's not the reason. I mean, you were just kids. You didn't know any better."

Then why had she even suggested it? Was she just being snarky, taking out her anger at Gram on Jane? Probably. But now that it had been said, it kept tracking through Jane's brain. She excused herself and carried her glass to the kitchen. Gram and Dad were just finishing up the dishes. He was describing the shipment of new pickup trucks that had arrived that day. Gram looked grateful for the interruption. Jane's dad never tired of talking pickup trucks. She said her good-byes, and her dad walked her out to her car, his arm draped across her shoulders.

"Seems something has you tense as an old transmission, baby. What's going on?"

Jane screwed up her courage and blurted out, "Do you think my unwillingness to accept Romeo as a step-dad had anything to do with him and Mom splitting up all those years ago?"

"What?" He released her. "Who put that fool idea into your pretty head?"

She didn't answer.

"Well, you just get it right on out of there. You hear me? That romance was a case of too hot too fast not to burn up like a pile of kindling."

Even with night creeping across the sky, she could see he was sincere. And his suggestion was one that hadn't occurred to her, but it was just as real a possibility as the one her mother had claimed and the one Vicky had suggested. She thanked him, hugged him, and left feeling better.

But once she was tucked into bed, her mind would not shut off. So instead of counting sheep, she imagined the ingredients needed for tomorrow's pie and counted those. *One mound of dough. Two pie tins. Three cups of blueberries.* Sleep began to pull her under, and Jane happily surrendered to its powerful seduction, praying there would be no dreams this night. *Four cups of sugar.*

Just as the last speck of awareness edged away, the Devil's image filled her mind's eye, and she heard her mother say, "Nick says you're coming around about the wedding." Her anger reignited, and there was no sleeping after that.

Chapter Seven

$\sim$

The smell of fresh coffee permeated the loft as Nick stepped from the shower and finished toweling off. Work awaited. He donned pajama bottoms and a T-shirt. The pj's had been a gift from Granna Anna, who hadn't approved of his sleeping in the nude. "Always keep some-a-thing to the imaginings." A smile tugged at the memory, and he wondered what she'd say if she knew he wore them only when he spent hours at the computer. Like tonight. He padded barefoot across the creaky wood floor, filled his mug, and added a healthy shot of Irish whiskey, then headed to his desk.

Night pressed against the windows, a mix of blackness and city lights that blinked and twinkled against the dark shadows of buildings and roof lines. The occasional threat to his peace and quiet came from the Broken Spur, a corner drinking hole, where hardcore boozers bellied up to the bar from noon until closing time, then stumbled out to their pickups with belligerent voices and squealing tires.

Usually he slept right through these disturbances. But on a hot summer night like this, he was glad for the air-conditioning that allowed him to leave the windows closed while he worked. He sank onto his chair, his gaze locked on the computer monitor, on Jane's face. The HD screen captured the gray flecks in the irises of her aqua eyes, the soft scar at the corner of one eyebrow that he had caused. His finger went to the screen as if he could touch it, trace it. She enthralled him. He couldn't get over how she'd changed, how photogenic she was. A photographer's dream subject. How could she not see that she was the hidden gem at the pie shop? That she should be the focus of the ad campaign?

Of course, Molly McCoy would be the face of the website. Big Sky Pie wouldn't exist without her acting on her vision. Plus, she was well known and respected in the community, and her pies were famous. People who didn't already know she had opened a pie shop would be delighted at the discovery. Business would boom. She was his ideal client: an everywoman entrepreneur with a universally popular product to sell. Piece of cake. Or in this case, slice of pie.

But the blog should be about the angel in the kitchen, and that title belonged to Jane. Although his memories of her were anything but angelic. Pure brat. With an angelic face. A vision of her seared across his mind's eye, a different version than the one on the monitor. This image wore specks of flour stuck to the corner of her mouth, that very kissable mouth.

He cleared his throat, shoving thoughts of seduction away, but as his gaze landed on the screen again, he realized he hadn't heard from her since yesterday. He was surprised how much he missed interacting with her, how much he missed being near her. What was wrong with him? This was the Pain. *And she's causing you a whole new kind of pain, Taz old boy.* He dragged his hand through his drying hair. She was more of a handful than he was used to, and damn, he liked that about her. His heart raced thinking about her curves.

He glanced at his phone, hoping she'd answered one of his texts, but she hadn't. If nothing else, she might have sent him a progress report on their secret investigation. God knew, he'd had no luck on that front. He'd also texted to remind her that he would be at the pie shop in the morning. He hoped she'd finally come to terms with that as it would make both of their jobs a hell of a lot easier.

Nick took a hefty swallow of his coffee, savoring the bite of the liquor, appreciating the mellow sensation it sent through his veins. He'd also texted Jane to inquire how her beautiful knees were doing, though he hadn't said *beautiful*, but he'd been tempted to, since she seemed to have serious self-esteem issues. He didn't understand why either. Didn't she realize that, with one kiss, a man couldn't get her out of his head or out from under his skin?

Why wasn't she answering his texts?

He glanced at the clock. Oh, hell, she was probably asleep. Great. Now images of Jane in bed plagued him. He wasn't going to accomplish much tonight if he couldn't stop picturing her with her strawberry hair splayed across her pillow, a sheet slipping low on her naked—the thought was interrupted by the outside door buzzer.

It was either some drunk or the pizza he'd ordered. He downed more coffee, then headed to the intercom. "Yeah?"

"Pizza."

"I'll be right there." He grabbed his wallet, then descended the stairs two at a time. As he approached the storefront door, he glimpsed a medium-height shadow through the obscure glass, a pizza box in hand. He undid the latch and froze.

Jane thrust the box into his chest, pushing past him and inside. "You owe me thirty dollars."

"The pizza only cost fifteen."

"You're a good tipper." She started up the stairs without another word and without limping. Obviously her knees felt better.

Smiling, Nick made sure the outer door was locked then hurried after her, clutching the pizza box, enjoying the long expanse of bare legs topped by a very short garment. She went into the loft and headed straight to the coffeepot, filled a mug, then asked, "Do you have anything to put in this? And I'm not talking sugar and cream."

"Bottle's right on the counter." He closed the loft door.

She spied the whiskey and poured some into the mug. Nick approached, drinking her in. She seemed to be wearing a raincoat over...nothing...and her hair was down, falling past her shoulders like a curly, reddish blond mass of silk.

He resisted the urge to shove his free hand into that inviting hair. He stopped two feet from her. "Figured you'd be asleep this time of night."

Her gaze went to the box. "Are you one of those guys who only likes pizza cold?"

He shrugged. What if he did like his pizza cold? He also liked it hot, and any temperature in between, but he doubted she gave a shit about that. "What's going on? Why did you traipse over here in your...your"—*whatever the hell you're wearing or not wearing under that*—"raincoat and those pink bunny slippers?"

She reached into his cupboard and yanked out a paper plate, tossing it at him. "Eat."

"I like it straight from the carton...like my milk." Her mouth puckered in distaste, and he smiled to himself as he flipped up the lid and pulled a slice free, offering it to her. "Join me?"

Jane recoiled. "No. I've eaten."

He set the box on the counter and bit into the meat lover's special, chewing slowly, hoping she could see he'd much rather be nibbling on her, all the while closing the gap between them to six tiny inches. She was backed against the counter, staring up at him, her gaze like a low blue flame.

"So what's going on, Pain? Have you taken a second

job as a sexy pizza deliverer come to seduce me with food and...fun?"

He stared at her mouth, letting her know he was definitely for that, if that was how he could accommodate her. He touched her hair, finding it as soft as he'd suspected, but that seemed a move too far. She slapped his hand away and pushed him back, but not before she'd revealed a flash of lust, of wanting. His thoughts started moving south. He retreated another step, ate another bite of pizza. "Maybe you'd rather tell me why you're here than let my imagination run wild."

He eyed a gap in her raincoat, mesmerized by a glimpse of creamy, ripe breasts.

She took a large gulp of steaming coffee and began choking. She covered her mouth with her hand and said a muffled, "Hot. Whiskey."

Nick handed her a fistful of napkins and sympathy, patting her back as she coughed. He'd lost his appetite. He dropped the pizza slice back into its box. He couldn't be this close to her and not think about what she was or was not wearing under that raincoat, and how to get her out of it and into his bed. Considering what he was wearing, he feared that was already pretty apparent. "Are you okay?"

"Like you care." She daubed at her face with a napkin, her look accusatory, like one she'd given him when they were kids, right after she'd gotten in trouble for breaking a vase that he had actually broken.

What had he done to her now? "Okay, you're upset,

and apparently I'm the cause, but I'm damned if I know why. You want to enlighten me?"

"I overheard what you and your dad said yesterday."

"Okay..." Nick shrugged, still as clueless as ever. "What did you overhear?"

Her aqua eyes were shooting daggers. "And then today my mom said the same thing to me."

"Are you going to tell me what you're talking about, or make me guess?"

Her hands landed on her hips, and the raincoat lifted higher on her bare thighs, spreading wider apart at the top, revealing even more alluring flesh. "About your little conspiracy to win me over to their side."

"Oh, shit." Nick rocked back, cringing hard, then pleading silently with her to believe him. "Oh, God. No. No, that is so not the case."

"You mean you didn't tell my mother and your father that you'd work on me?"

He groaned. "Look, I had a lot to drink at the engagement party. I don't recall most of the later part of the evening. I had to call a cab to get home."

"I don't hear a denial in there." She lifted her mug, but this time took a tiny sip.

"I don't remember making any such pact with our parents, but apparently...they think I did."

"And you have done nothing since to clear up the misunderstanding?"

"Well, no, but I told you how I feel about their upcoming marriage."

"But you're not man enough to tell them."

"Let's not drag my manhood into this."

"Why not? You've been using it to try and seduce me. Kissing me senseless so I'll capitulate and give our parents my blessing."

"Any attempts at seduction on my part have nothing to do with our parents." His gaze landed on her lush lips, his breath hitching, his voice dropping to a low rumble. "Blame that on your kissable mouth."

Jane gave a defiant toss of her silken hair, scenting the air with something flowery, and Nick nearly lost it. He wanted to sweep her into his arms, let her see exactly how crazed she was making him, but he forced himself to stand where he was, fighting the sexual tug, looking at her, wanting her, and worried that he might be losing his mind feeling this way about the Pain.

* * *

"You find my mouth kissable?" Jane asked on a laugh, not believing for a minute that he did. She held his gaze as she gave Nick what she hoped was a smoldering look. She was no seductress. She'd only ever had sex twice, and both times she'd found it unsatisfying, awkward, and messy. But this seduction wouldn't be going that far. It would be more like a tease-fest, just enough foreplay to get his juices really pumping, without any real pumping. She closed the gap between them, needing Nick within easy reach. Her plan required intimate contact. Nick seemed only too happy to oblige.

Shivers flashed through her, some delicious, some apprehensive, and she had to keep reminding herself that he deserved this. He needed to know what it felt like to have his emotions jerked around and upside down. He'd been playing her, was still playing her. Andrea claimed a dose of his own medicine was the only cure for a man who toyed with women's affections.

At the time, Jane thought it sounded like a great idea, something easily carried off. Since Nick seemed so intent on seducing her, she figured he would do most of the work for her. She just wanted him really hot and bothered, and then she'd break it off. But given her shy nature, launching the seduction had her nervous and dry mouthed. Why wasn't he taking the initiative like he always did? After all, she hardly had any clothes on. Jane blushed. That was actually an accident. She'd just been so ticked off that she'd jumped out of bed and thrown on her raincoat, without any thought to her state of undress, but being near-naked should be working in her favor.

So why wasn't it? Why did she get so heated when he stood this close, when the only thing touching her was his sensuous gaze, when his citrusy scent awakened natural pheromones, loosening her inhibitions. Her tongue darted out, and Nick emitted a feral groan, finally moving, finally touching her. He reached over and traced his thumb along her bottom lip. Her body responded with a rush of liquid heat and an ache to be in his arms.

What was wrong with her? He was supposed to be the one succumbing to her sexual charms, not the other way around. But as his mouth descended onto hers and took full possession, all thoughts of revenge slipped into the abyss.

He pulled her to him. The thin cloth of his pajama bottoms left no doubt of his arousal. He wanted her. Bad. It was the last clear thought Jane had as the kiss began to boggle her mind, and her body took over. A loud roaring started in her ears, and then the building seemed to rock as though struck by a tornado, catching her in a vortex of desire that spun with such speed that she couldn't extract herself if she wanted to. She didn't want to.

No man had ever touched her like this, made her feel this abandon, this crazed need that had her tearing at Nick's clothing. It was like something she'd seen in movies, a couple so impassioned they couldn't get at each other fast enough, possessed by a physical and emotional ardor that blocked out reason and free will. Clothing flew in all directions, naked skin collided, and the next thing Jane knew, she was on his bed with Nick above her, his eyes fevered, his mouth a thing of delicious torture.

Until this moment, she hadn't understood why people raved about the joys of sex, hadn't ever experienced a jarring climax, but as Nick entered her, hot, hard, and thrilling, fireworks seemed to burst through her. Almost immediately, she felt the next fuse lighting, igniting, the friction building toward another rapturous explosion, her pleasure increasing with his frenzied thrusts, until ecstasy burst through her.

Jane struggled to catch her breath. Nick seemed to be

doing the same. He raised himself to peer into her eyes, his hair falling over his forehead, a crooked smile forming. "What the hell was that?"

The question was as sobering as a bucket of ice water. Jane could not explain what had just happened to herself, let alone to him. What the hell had she just done? Slept with the Devil, that's what. Oh, my God. She was only supposed to half seduce him, make him stop flirting with her for all the wrong reasons. But something else had seemed to possess her. She had to get out of here. Where were her panties?

Nick caught her wrist as she started to stand. "Hey, where are you going?"

She fought her embarrassment, covered herself with her hands, suddenly not the sex goddess she'd felt like moments ago. "It was sex, Nick. That's all. Thanks for satisfying my curiosity."

"Bull. That wasn't just sex."

"Sure it was. It's not like we're falling for each other. I don't even like you." She spied her panties and tugged them on, quickly donning her raincoat and stuffing her feet into her slippers.

She saw Nick's amused eyes go to the fuzzy pink bunny slippers. She tossed him his pajama bottoms. "Cover yourself."

"You didn't seem to mind this sight a few minutes ago."

Jane rolled her eyes as he shoved off the bed and drew on his pj's, as another jolt of reality hit her. They hadn't used protection. The last thing she'd wanted was to make their relationship more of a mess than it was. She had to work with this man. She might even end up related to him by marriage again. And he was a liar and a player, and she had never been more humiliated and embarrassed.

She raced into the other room for her purse. Her face was so hot it probably flashed brighter than the neon signage on the Broken Spur Saloon. She ran for the door.

Nick was yanking on his pajama bottoms as he chased after her but she reached the stairs first and fled.

* * *

Nick raced after Jane, but couldn't catch up. When he reached the bottom landing, the outer door was just closing. The latch caught with a loud clack. Except for his rapid breath, silence echoed throughout the hallway and then fell over him. The sensation was so eerie that he might have only imagined she'd been there, but then he spied it, just inside the door.

One fuzzy pink bunny slipper.

Chapter Eight

I don't like to speak ill of the dead," BiBi said, glancing up from the recipes she'd spread across one end of the work counter. "Especially when they're still alive, but Jane, you have serious zombie eyes."

Jane, finishing the last of the crusts for that day's pies, squinted at her assistant. "Zombie eyes?"

"Yeah, ginormous black circles." She stroked under one of her perfectly made-up baby blues for emphasis and grinned. "Walk of shame eyes, like on *RDOHMs*."

Jane had no idea what those initials stood for, but knowing her assistant it had something to do with a television show and men. She guessed the show might be something like: *Randy Dudes of Horse Mountain*. Grandma Wilson's words about flaky women sprang to mind.

BiBi was grinning at her lasciviously. "Anything you should be confessing? Say . . . a wild ride on a hot cowboy every night this week?"

"No." Jane sucked in a breath, but a guilty blush flooded her cheeks as she recalled the wild ride she'd shared with Nick seven days earlier. What had she been thinking? It couldn't ever happen again. Even if tantalizing memories of their lovemaking haunted her dreams. She muttered, "Nothing like that."

"Hmm, well, I was sure that you must have been booty-shaking your nights away in some kick-ass, sex-me pumps from the way you've favored your left foot since last week."

"I stepped on some broken glass, but it's almost healed." The lie wasn't that far-fetched; the sole of her foot had looked and felt like she'd done just that. Jane finished crimping the last edge of crust, biting her tongue to keep from asking her assistant why she couldn't apply that keen sense of observation to baking pies. Perhaps then she wouldn't be relegated to making the pies for the pie-eating contest, where only taste, not presentation, mattered.

"So I thought that sexy ex-stepbrother of yours was supposed to be here all week getting the advertising stuff ready for the open house, but unless he's coming in after I've gone home, I haven't seen him. Have you?"

No, thank God. Just the mention of Nick sent a shiver through Jane. She carried the pies to the waiting ovens. Her zombie eyes were his fault. "I heard he had to go to Vegas to help his dad clear up some last-minute details having to do with the sale of his dad's limousine business. Not sure when they'll be back in town." It would be too soon for Jane whenever it was.

BiBi released a sigh full of disappointment. "Pity. I was looking forward to discussing my ideas for advertising the pie-eating contest with him."

"Why don't you start slicing some butter cubes?" Jane cleaned the marble work counter and pulled out the food processors and supplies to make the dough mounds they would need tomorrow. "Isn't Callee coming in to discuss the pie-eating contest advertising with you in a little while?"

"Yeah, but she's no Nick Taziano." BiBi pulled bars of butter from the freezer, carried them to the counter, and dug out a knife and cutting board. "If we were running a contest at the grand opening for, say, a Mr. Delicious, he'd win hands down."

"Mr. Delicious?" Jane laughed. "Nick?"

"Yes, Nick. One look and my mouth waters every time."

"If you say so." Jane shook her head, but her body heated from the inside out at just how melt-in-your-mouth-yummy he was. She had firsthand knowledge. Carnal knowledge. Images assailed her: Nick in pj's and a T-shirt, Nick teasing her, Nick kissing her, Nick making love to her. Okay, so he *was* delicious. He was also an ass.

She placed the flour and butter into the food processor and added a teaspoon of ice water. It was his fault her half-seduction turned into mind-blowing sex that she couldn't not stop recalling. A second wave of heat spread into her cheeks. She hit the pulse button once, twice, three times, and then added more water.

He'd cast his devil's spell on her, turning her will to his, burning her inhibitions like tissue paper. That was humiliating enough, but then she'd fled like some deflowered Cinderella, losing her slipper in the process. She was an idiot, a cliché.

She deserved a wounded foot for bad judgment.

BiBi interrupted her dark thoughts. "Look, Jane, is there something going on between you and Nick?"

Jane couldn't look her in the eye. "No, nothing." *Pulse. Pulse.*

"Then you wouldn't mind if I...you know...get to know him better?"

The question dripped with sexual innuendo and drove an unexpected zing of jealousy through Jane. "Nick and I are..." What were they? Ex-stepsiblings? Frienemies? Lovers? No. Nothing, that's what. *Pulse. Pulse. Pulse.* "You don't need my permission."

"Okay, I didn't want to step on your toes, you know?" BiBi's smile held a touch of anticipation that irked Jane. "Hey, aren't you overpulsing that dough?"

Jane blanched and lifted her finger from the pulse button. The mixture seemed okay. She would know once she worked with it. She spread a thin layer of flour on the counter and dumped the loose dough mixture onto it, then began gently smooshing it into a solid mound. "What pies are you considering for the pie-eating contest?"

"Hmm..." BiBi diced butter, her thinking cap as visible as if it were a beanie. *She isn't even thinking about recipes*, Jane realized, *but about what's going on with me*. And she wouldn't quit guessing until she'd pried out every detail. Jane groaned to herself as BiBi said, "If the yummy Nick isn't responsible for those zombie eyes, is it that you're still stressing about your mom?"

Jane's stomach lurched at how close this nail had come to being hit on the head. She didn't answer. She patted the dough into a mound and started another. She wanted to tell her assistant that she wasn't getting paid to stick her nose where it wasn't welcome. But how could she? She'd invited it by confiding in her the other day. Suddenly saying "It's none of your business" wasn't going to cut it. "Yeah, I suppose."

"I knew it. I'm telling you, *RDOHM*."

Jane glanced at her over the food processor. "I have no idea what the hell that even is."

BiBi's mouth dropped open. "*Real Daughters of Hollywood Moguls.* I can't believe you've missed it. It's the hottest show on cable right now. You need to tune in. Ariel Magnus Wittendale has almost exactly the same shit going on with her parents that you have with yours. And her mom is about to remarry one of her loser exes. It's like you and Ariel are sisters of the heart, except that Ariel is richer than Oprah and... you're, well... not."

"Ariel who?"

"Oh, my God, Jane." BiBi gaped. "You're hopeless. Ivor Magnus Wittendale owns iMagnus Studios. How could you not know that? It's like you live in a cave."

"I don't watch reality shows." The public's fascination with other people's misery eluded Jane. She'd seen too much of her mother's suffering to want to peek into the private lives of others, especially since so much of it was scripted arguments and phony angst, like mean girls gone viral. "Those shows are as fake as your tattoo."

BiBi touched the sticker on her neck. "I'm testing this design, living with it until I decide if I want to make it permanent."

More like you want Daddy's approval first. But Jane regretted the comment; talk about mean girls. Taking her bad mood out on BiBi was beneath her, unkind and undeserved. She waved her hand. "I'm sorry, BiBi. Please, ignore me. I'm just tired."

Still BiBi wouldn't let it drop. "Haven't you spoken to your mother since the engagement party?"

"I have," Jane said. She finished wrapping the last of the mounds and placed them into the Sub-Zero, then she washed her hands. The warm water and gentle soap cleansed bits of clinging dough from between her fingers and under her nails, but the harshest soap, the hottest water, could not scrub away the guilt stalking her. How could she tell her mother to stay away from Romeo when she'd had the same reaction to his son? Oh, she wasn't in love with Nick, but lusting for him was close enough to it to scare the hell out of her. "I'm not sure what to do."

"Can't you just tell her how you're feeling?"

Hardly. She couldn't confess to her mom that she'd fallen into Nick's bed with total abandon. But feeling as she did, how could she come to terms with his being "family" again? She couldn't. There would never be a single comfortable holiday together. This was a mess.

Plus her sense that her mother was making a huge mistake seemed stronger than ever. Or was it now just twisted and tangled up with how she felt about Nick? She didn't know. If only there was an impartial someone she could talk to...

Jane caught BiBi's expression and knew she was eagerly awaiting some kind of response, but her assistant was no longer someone she could confide in, given BiBi's confessed feelings for Nick. Thankfully, the tap-tapping of heels entering the kitchen saved Jane from saying anything.

Callee strolled in wearing a summer dress, denim jacket, and red Dingos. Sunlight caught in her bouncy hair and matched her sunny greeting. "Jane, that couple I was telling you about yesterday, the ones who want to have pie at their wedding reception?"

"Yes." Jane nodded. She hadn't forgotten. She'd brought along an extra freshly pressed chef coat for the meeting, but given her mental state, she'd rather jump in a pile of mud than deal with a giddy engaged couple. She asked with more hope in her voice than she meant, "Have they canceled?"

"No." Callee laughed. "They'll be here very soon. Andrea will handle the meeting, but I'd like you to walk the clients through the pie samples. I need to go over the grand opening advertising with BiBi."

"Sure." She could discuss pies with anyone. It was selling a service to customers she wanted no part of. "The sample platter is ready and waiting in the display case."

"You are a wonder." Callee clearly liked that her employees stepped up without even being asked. "Now, go into the café, get a cup of coffee, and get off your feet for a little while."

"Thank you. I think I will." Right after I freshen up a bit.

Callee turned her attention to BiBi. "I can't wait to hear your ideas for the pie-eating contest and share what I'm thinking for the advertising."

"I've been doing all kinds of research," BiBi said, her voice bright with self-pride. "Did you know there's a World Pie Eating Championship? The competition is held every year in Wigan, England."

Jane went into the bathroom, fixed her hair, worked to rid herself of the zombie eyes, and exchanged her dirty chef coat with the clean one.

When she came out into the kitchen, BiBi was chattering excitedly. "Pie-eating contests used to be about who could consume the most pies, but given the appetite of some of the cowboys around here, we'd be baking pies for a month. Not to mention the risk of someone ending up in the ER from overindulgence. I suggest we go with a timed competition. That's whoever can consume one whole pie in the fastest time wins."

"I like that," Callee said. "I'm really pleased with how you're handling this, BiBi."

BiBi beamed at the praise. "Jane suggested we do a sweet pie since flavor will be more important to the contestants than presentation. Nothing sells pies faster than word of mouth, and so we should have some of our usual pies with the same filling we use for the contest pies. And I'm thinking this month's specialty. Blueberry is pretty universal in appeal. But my recipe for the contest pies differs from Molly's. I heat the berries before putting them in the pie dough. It keeps the berries from getting too gooey."

"You are really on top of this." Callee withdrew some sheets of paper from a manila envelope she'd brought. "I've been working on some ideas for the look of the advertising and have some thoughts about the reward. What do you think of one grand prize winner and two runner-ups?"

Jane liked how Callee included BiBi in the decision making, respecting her ideas and offering her own as suggestions, not stipulations. She left them, heads bent over the paperwork, and went into the café. Andrea was bussing empty tables; gathering silverware, dessert dishes, and cups and saucers onto a wheeled cart; and bidding departing customers a good evening. Jane doubted Andrea's job description included straightening the café, but she seemed to always pitch in where needed.

There was a pair of middle-aged women in one of the booths, lingering over slices of the blueberry cream pie, and a guy on a computer at the table near the bay windows. Jane grabbed a cup of coffee and settled at the end booth, the only permanently reserved spot in the café. Quint had commandeered it as a temporary office until his mama returned to take charge of her business. Andrea had already laid out brochures on the table.

Jane sank onto the deep cushions with a sigh and pulled her phone from her pocket. She scanned missed calls, messages, and texts. Most were from her mother. She still had not given her an answer about being her maid of honor. What was she going to do? To say? It kept coming back to how she felt about Romeo.

"Mind if I join you?" Andrea said, setting a cup of coffee on the table and sliding into the booth across from Jane. "You look like you could use a girlfriend about now. I'm a good listener."

In a lot of ways, Andrea reminded Jane of Rebel, the provocative way she dressed, her sharp sense of humor, outgoing nature, and her natural beauty. *The complete opposite of me.* But now that she'd gotten to know her better, she realized that Andrea and she shared a commonality. They both had had to grow up and take charge at a young age, Andrea for the sake of her two little boys, Jane for the sake of a mother who was often more child than parent.

"I'm just tired," Jane said, using the same line she'd given BiBi earlier in the day. It wasn't a lie. She could almost hear her bed calling.

"I kind of thought it had something to do with your mom."

Jane looked up from her phone. Had her assistant been gossiping to Andrea? "Why would you think that?"

"Sorry, I can read upside down, something I perfected while working as Quint's real estate office manager. You'd be surprised how often it proved a handy talent. Anyway, I noticed that you've got your mom on speed dial, but you seem to be trying to decide whether or not to hit Send."

Jane set her phone aside and took a sip of coffee, so torn about how she felt that she couldn't even express it.

"Does it have something to do with her marrying Nick's dad again?"

Did the whole town know about that? Of course they did. It was in the papers. Plus, Andrea and Callee and Quint were good friends. She was sure they all had an opinion about it that differed from her own. "I want to be happy for her but I'm not sure how I feel. I can't shake the sense that she shouldn't remarry this man. And I can't tell if it's instinct or my long-held dislike of him."

Andrea tucked her thick blond hair behind one ear, revealing a dangling earring, her gaze sympathetic. "As women, we often ignore our instincts when we shouldn't. Can you discuss this with your mom?"

"Maybe. If she hadn't already married a few wrong-for-her men, and if I hadn't had a talk with her on each of those occasions. I'm afraid she'll think it's more of the same."

"Hmm." Andrea sipped some coffee, then said, "Could you hold off on the talk and spend a couple of afternoons or evenings with them, observing them together? Test your instincts? See how he treats your mom? Then if you still feel the same way, have the talk?"

The suggestion was like someone placing stepping-stones across a swiftly moving stream, providing dry passage from one side to the other, the solution so simple she should have thought of it herself. "That is such a great idea. Thank you, Andrea."

She would start to implement the plan tonight by phoning her mother as soon as she left work today. The key would be keeping an open mind about Nick's dad.

"Good, you're already looking less stressed." Andrea laughed.

The bell over the door sounded. Jane glanced up to see a white-haired couple wearing floral shirts in a splash of colors trundle in. Andrea got up to greet and seat them, but Jane heard the woman proclaim, "We have an appointment with Ms. McCoy to discuss hiring Big Sky Pie to cater our wedding reception."

Jane slipped out of the booth, straightening her chef coat with damp palms. Although she was required only to serve the pie samples and answer questions related to the samples, she couldn't quell her anxiety. Selling herself and, in this case, the pie shop's catering services drew old insecurities to the surface. Callee and Andrea had placed so much trust in her, and she didn't want to let them down. What if this couple hated her pies? Taste was subjective, after all, and there were bound to be people who preferred other pies to hers.

Andrea gestured toward the end booth, where she'd laid out the catering brochures for them to browse. She and Jane brought them coffee, and Andrea made the introductions. "Jane, this is Betty and Dean Gardener."

They acknowledged her with the friendliness of two happy puppies, excited to share their day with anyone who crossed their path. Jane's anxiety eased. She retreated to a nearby table, where she could watch, and learn, without being a distraction, as Andrea discussed the various catering plans. She soon realized there was a joy about this man and woman—about their shy touches and blissful smiles—that filled the room with cheer, brightening the darkest corners, and lifting the weightiness of a long day from Jane's tired muscles. Even her coffee tasted sweeter, although it contained no sugar. *This must be what love feels like, looks like. Did her mother and Romeo look like this?* She hadn't even noticed.

"Why don't you tell me a little about yourselves and your wedding reception?" Andrea asked, taking notes.

Betty and Dean exchanged smiles, then Betty said, "We met in high school. Forty years ago. Dean was my first love."

"That's amazing." The wonder in Andrea's voice spoke volumes about her own lack of success marrying a high school sweetheart. "So this wedding is a renewal-of-vows ceremony and reception?"

"Where'd you get that idea?" Dean asked, his scraggy eyebrows lifting. "We've never been married...to each other."

"But you said—"

"You see, back then, our parents objected," Betty said, a note of bitterness in her voice. "Said we were too young."

"In those days, good kids did what their parents told them to do." Dean placed his hand over Betty's, the gesture striking Jane as comforting, protective. "They threatened to send Betty away if I didn't steer clear of her. So I joined the army and was sent overseas."

Betty swallowed hard, a sheen of tears in her eyes. "I promised Dean I'd wait for him forever. And I would have, too, but we got word he'd died in Vietnam."

The tremor of pain in her voice grabbed hold of Jane's heart. She'd never experienced a first love, unless she counted Trent Andrews in junior high, but the teenage crush hadn't had her committing to a lifetime with him. She couldn't even imagine the devastating heartbreak of thinking the man she loved had died.

"I was taken prisoner," Dean said on a bitter, strident laugh. "Nearly did die in that war camp."

Betty gave him a quick kiss on the cheek. "After a couple of years passed, I married someone else, but I never stopped loving and missing my Dean."

I never got over him. Although falling in love and getting married were not what Jane wanted for herself, she understood just how difficult and messy life could be, and she was starting to see that the road to love already had enough pitfalls and potholes without family interference making it worse.

"I married a couple of someone elses, too," Dean said. "But none of 'em was my Betty."

Betty blushed and giggled. "Finally, we were both single at the same time, and when he called, well, let's just say this time nobody is going to stop us from being together."

"Amen." Dean bumped the table with his fist like a judge pounding a gavel to make his point.

The lyrics to a Trisha Yearwood song played through Jane's mind, about things that were meant to be finding a way, about a couple who would, despite all obstacles, be married one day. *Like Mom and Romeo?* Her conscience tickled. Was she—and maybe Nick—as intolerant and misguided as Dean and Betty's parents? The possibility bothered her.

"We own the new florist shop out by the hospital. The Flower Garden. We know the name isn't that original, but it's a play off Dean's last name and my maiden name, Flowers," Betty giggled again. "We're doing the flowers for our own wedding, of course, but we'd be glad for any recommendations if you wouldn't mind. We could use the business."

Jane made a mental note to mention their shop to her mother.

The bell over the door sounded. Jane glanced up, her thoughts so focused on her mother that she wouldn't have been surprised to see Rebel coming into the shop. But it was Nick.

Her heart skipped and skidded. God, he was so handsome, tall, tanned, his grin showcased by those devilish dimples. His shirt hugged his taut belly, scuffed boots poked from beneath his worn blue jeans, and a camera hung from a belt loop. Mr. Delicious. Her tongue slipped across her lips, and her gaze snagged on something he was holding behind his back.

Something pink and fuzzy.

Chapter Nine

*T*he smell. *Sweet. Spicy. Tantalizing.*

It hit Nick every time he walked into Big Sky Pie, a smack to the olfactory senses that could knock out whatever bothered a man and infuse him with a feeling of arriving at a safe haven. A reinforcement of the old adage about the way to a man's heart being through his stomach. His taste buds watered in anticipation.

Until his gaze collided with Jane's, then his gut did a slow roll, and his mouth went drier than the Mojave. When had just looking at her started to take his breath away? And how did he make it stop? She was the last woman he wanted to be attracted to. They didn't even like each other. They didn't share the same goals. He was not going to get involved with another woman who was all wrong for him. Oh, why had he slept with her? It shouldn't have happened. Now he couldn't look at her without wanting to do it again, and again. He couldn't get her out of his head.

He wasn't sure how she would react when she saw him, but her expression made him regret whatever impulse had thought it was a good idea to return her slipper to her at the pie shop. Man, what was he thinking? Why hadn't he at least put it into a shopping bag? Presenting one fuzzy pink bunny slipper to her was bound to demand an explanation to her coworkers, which in turn would embarrass Jane and put him at the top of her shit list.

If he wasn't there already.

He tried tucking it behind him, but it was too late. She'd already seen it, her beautiful eyes narrowing as if to convey he was lucky there were no lethal weapons at hand—although she might choose to stab him with one of the dessert forks on the table. "Jane, could you come outside for a minute?"

The shop was so quiet that he hadn't realized they weren't alone, until Andrea peeked out of the end booth, and then a white-haired stranger did the same. A second later, Nick realized he knew this stranger. "Dean Gardener, hey, how are you?"

"Fine, Nick. Couldn't be better." Dean rose from the booth, hand extended for a shake. And Nick accommodated, the reflex automatic, but instead of taking his hand, Dean chuckled. "What the hell is that?"

Nick had extended the hand holding the fuzzy pink bunny slipper. The collar of his shirt felt buttoned tight and two sizes too small. He switched the slipper to his empty hand and shook with Dean. "It's nothing. Forgot I was holding it."

"Thought maybe it was a new camera cover," Dean teased.

Nick laughed, pretending not to see the unspoken questions in Andrea's and Betty's eyes, pretending not to hear the slight choking sound Jane made behind him. What exactly had he stumbled into anyway? He took in the brochures, recalled the pie samples and dessert plates and forks on Jane's table, and it dawned on him. He'd just barreled through a catering meeting.

But before he could apologize, Dean said, "Are you doing the advertising for the pie shop, Nick?"

Nick had set up a website and done an advertising campaign for the Flower Garden a few months back. "I am."

"Then you might want to take some photos of us. We're considering booking Big Sky Pie for our wedding reception. We've been meaning to speak to you about updating our website with our wedding preparations, and we'd love to have a photo of us picking out our pie for the reception."

Nick grabbed at the chance to undo any harm his poorly timed arrival might have caused. "Then you've made up your mind to hire Big Sky Pie?"

"Thinking about it," Dean said.

"Think no more. You won't be disappointed," Nick enthused. "I can recommend the pies. Best in the state and beyond."

"Well, in that case," Dean said to Andrea, "where do we sign?"

"Don't you want to taste the pie samples first?" Andrea appeared a bit taken back by the sudden turn of events, but she was smiling.

"Not necessary. If Nick Taziano recommends you, it's good enough for us."

Jane seemed less happy. In fact, Nick could almost see the hair on her neck bristling. Why? Hadn't he just done them a favor by securing the shop's first wedding event? Hell, yes, he had.

"We do want to taste the samples, Andrea," Betty said, then added to her fiancé, "We still need to decide which flavors we'd like for the reception, Dean."

"Well, sure. I've been looking forward to that part. The aroma in this place has got my stomach growling."

Andrea refilled their coffee cups and handed the pie tasting over to Jane.

Nick ignored Jane's "I don't need your help" glower and assisted her in transferring dessert plates and silverware to the booth table, whispering under his breath, "When you're done here, please wait for me. I'd like to talk to you..."

"Go away," Jane whispered, then focused her attention on Dean and Betty.

Nick left the slipper where she could see it, poured himself a mug of coffee, and headed into the kitchen for his meeting with Callee and BiBi.

Half an hour later, the advertising meeting over, he returned to the café to find the slipper where he'd left it and Jane gone. Guilt spiked through him. He owed her an apology and an explanation. In the week he'd been in Vegas with his dad, he'd had a revelation. His whole outlook had shifted, giving him a clear vision of his future. And of his past. Like it or not, Jane's and his lives were going to be intertwined, professionally and personally, for a long time. If he could make amends to her, set things straight between them, then maybe they could go forward without a lot of awkwardness.

He took the slipper and was standing on her doorstep a little while later, ringing the bell. She didn't answer, but he knew she was in there. Her Jeep occupied its parking space, and he could hear movement near the door. "Come on, Jane, I really need to talk to you."

"Go away." The words had a finality that suggested she never wanted to talk to, or see, him again. *She wished.*

"I have something that belongs to you." He held the slipper up to the peephole.

From behind the door, he heard her mutter, "Shit."

The door cracked open, and her hand snaked out. Nick said, "Oh, no you don't. Not until we talk."

"Then keep it." She started to slam the door.

He stuck his foot on the threshold. "Maybe you'd rather I shout what I have to say through the door, then all the neighbors can hear?"

It was a lame threat, but apparently she thought he'd actually do that. The door opened wider. She looked fresh from a shower, her strawberry blond hair down, damp, and curling around her cheeks. Very pink cheeks. She was either furious or embarrassed or a combination of both. She wore a skimpy aqua top that floated around her plump breasts and Daisy Duke cutoffs that drew his attention to her long legs and bare feet with nails painted a sunny orange. He wanted to grab her, hold her, kiss her, and bury himself deep inside her.

He fought the urges and apologized for taking the slipper to the pie shop without first putting it into a shopping bag. "I just didn't think."

Her expression suggested that was his usual mental condition. "You could have just left it on my apartment stoop."

"Jane, we can't act like what happened between us didn't." He closed the door, his gaze locked with hers. "We made love."

"No. We had sex." The pink in her cheeks went scarlet. "It was need, pure and simple. Two consenting adults indulging a mutual attraction. Nothing more."

Nick couldn't help himself; he grinned. "It was amazing."

Despite his determination not to touch her, he found his fingers reaching toward her hair. She reared back, warning him off. "It was a mistake."

"Agreed," he said, although her feeling that way, too, drove disappointment into his heart. "But it was still amazing."

She blushed that blood-stirring blush. "It shouldn't have happened. We didn't even use protection. God knows who all you've slept with and what kind of STD I'm at risk for now."

His brows lifted, and his grin widened. "You can stop worrying about that. I'm clean."

She actually looked relieved. She'd probably be shocked to discover he wasn't the hound dog she seemed to think he was. Not that she'd likely believe it. "Jane, I won't deny that I'd like nothing better than to pursue whatever this attraction is between us." *So much so it's killing me not to kiss you right now.* "But I'm sorry I took advantage."

He didn't look sorry. She dragged a hand through her hair, ran her tongue over her lips, and looked at her bare feet. It took every ounce of willpower in him not to take back his words, not to touch her. She glanced up, contrition in her eyes. "It wasn't all your fault."

They stared at each other, and the air seemed to sizzle with a sexual magnetism that spiked through Nick's veins and robbed his breath. He grappled with the urge to give in to his desire. He could not allow this conversation to end up in her bed. He said nothing. Just nodded.

Jane licked her lips again, those damned kissable lips. She said, "If you were anyone else...this wouldn't be uncomfortable..."

"It doesn't need to be...if we don't let it." Had he really just said that? Were they really going to be this grown-up? Did they have a choice?

"Okay. Then we agree. No more intimate contact."

"I can do that." But could he? He had to.

"Good." She lifted her hair from her shoulders and let it fall in a gesture of relief. "I'm glad you understand. But then, I guess you would, wouldn't you? You were about my age when you started your career. You know the dedication that's required to take it to the next level and the next."

Nick did know what was required. He'd given up a lot of personal fulfillment to get his business on track.

Jane said, "My mom always told me not to take my eyes off the prize, not to fall for some guy and then lose track of what I planned for my life. Big Sky Pie is a great starting point for me, but once I have some serious experience under my belt and have saved enough money, I intend to live in France. I want to attend a top pastry school and work there for a couple of years before I come home and start my own pastry shop. I don't have time to fall in love with anyone."

"And I do want to fall in love with someone." But for many reasons that someone was not Jane. Nick rubbed his jaw. Whatever this pull was between them, it was definitely not love. Lust for sure, but not love. He needed to take a page from Jane's book, to keep his eye on his end goal. A wife and kids, a house with a swing in the backyard. "I'm tired of being single."

"Not me." She made a face and headed to the refrigerator.

Nick watched the gentle sway of her hips, and images of those long, smooth legs wrapped around him heated his blood. Damn it. He had to get control of himself. Stop thinking of her like this. He forced his gaze elsewhere, walked to the window, and stared out at the view. The yard below had, ironically, a swing set with a couple of kids playing on it. *Eyes on the prize.* "The trip with Dad to Vegas was an eye-opener."

"Oh?" She pulled a couple of Mike's Hard Lemonades from the refrigerator and brought one to him. "It's not beer, but it's cold and refreshing on a hot afternoon like this."

"Thanks." He took a long swig.

Jane sipped at hers. "Did you find out why your dad and my mother divorced?"

He lowered the bottle and ran a hand across his head. "I found out that Dad and my mother were never married."

Jane's brows lifted slightly, then she shrugged. "You never knew that?"

"I don't think they ever told anyone. People assumed, and they let them."

"Well, I doubt anyone cared." She scooted onto the wide windowsill, crossing her legs, drawing his eye there. "A lot of couples live together without taking that trip down the aisle. I wish my mother had opted to just live with some of the guys she married. God knows, I've tried convincing her that love doesn't require a legal stamp of approval."

"My parents didn't love each other."

A soft gasp escaped Jane, and her eyes widened, filling with something akin to the shock that Nick had felt when his dad told him this, but words seemed to fail her, so Nick said, "Yep, I was a surprise. Apparently, they met in the Middle East while Dad was in the last month of his stint in the army. She was a freelance photojournalist. They hooked up for a few days, then went their separate ways."

"And..."

"And a month or two after Dad came back to Kalispell, Mom showed up to tell him she was pregnant. He offered to marry her on the spot, but she didn't want to be tied down to anyone, not even me."

Jane seemed to swallow hard, and she took a step toward him. "I'm sorry, Nick."

Nick nodded, then gulped some of his icy drink and wiped his mouth with his forearm. "Dad made a deal with her. He took legal and physical custody of me, and she used our house as her home base whenever she was in the States. As a kid, I took her absences as work and didn't think anything about it until I started school and realized that other kids' mothers didn't have work that took them away from home for months or years at a time."

He took another drink. "I began to resent her work, to grow more and more angry with her. One night I blew up and tore my room apart. That's when Dad sat me down and told me that her job helped out the victims of war, little boys and girls less fortunate than me, helping them to find food and shelter. In my child's mind, she became a hero, larger than life, the greatest mother of all time, but in fact, she was just a restless soul who was only truly content in the middle of conflict-torn countries, recording travesties and inhumanities."

Jane touched his arm in comfort, but said nothing. He didn't look at her, didn't want to see pity in her lovely eyes. "She died when she stepped on a land mine. In my mind, she went from hero to saint. I was

ten. It was all I had to cling to. That and my dad.
But the truth is, Mom wasn't a hero. She took foolish
chances for the sake of a photograph, a magazine arti-
cle. She chose her career over her child. I didn't know
that, though, when Dad fell in love with Rebel. I never
gave your mom a chance to be a stepmother to me. I
resented her before I met her. She couldn't ever live up
to the 'mother image' in my head. And she was taking
my only parent from me."

"You think you and I broke up their marriage?"

"Dad didn't say, but given these new facts about my
childhood and some recent memories about the year
from hell, I can believe we might have been major con-
tributors." He sighed. "I'm not going to fight their marriage anymore, Jane."

She pressed her lips together and nodded. "I came to
that same conclusion today after listening to what happened to Dean and Betty Gardener."

Nick downed more of his drink, glad that he'd opened
up, glad that neither of them would stand in the way
of their parents' reunion. "This is the biggest reason I
regret our night together. Since we're going to be stepsiblings again, I don't want you to feel uncomfortable in
my company." If only he could scrub the memories from
his brain, but he couldn't, damn it. Nor could he stop
yearning for her.

"As long as it doesn't happen again, then I can deal."
She issued it like a challenge, like she didn't trust him to
stick to his word.

He wanted her to understand how serious he was.

"When I walked away from Dad's limo service in Vegas and came back here to start my own business, I did it without any financial help from him. He could have been my largest advertising account, my bread and butter, but I wanted to make it on my own. You know?"

She laughed. "I did the same thing with my mother's wedding-planning business. She wanted me to join her, but I had to follow my own heart, my own path. I want to make it on my own, too."

"I know you do." He respected her for that and knew that he mustn't do anything to cause her to veer from that goal. He would never forgive himself if he did. Nick stared at the swing set as if it were a touchstone reminding him of his own goals. "I've spent a lot of years on the road, chasing clients, and it's growing old. The travel makes having any real personal life almost impossible. Plus I don't have anything to prove anymore. So there was no longer any reason not to do the advertising for my dad's business, if he still wanted me to. But before I approached him about that, I decided to work up an ad campaign for him. My timing was off. I didn't get a chance to show it to him before he sold the limo service and retired. But when we were in Vegas this past week tying up loose ends with the company..." He scratched his head, not really sure how it had happened, but glad that it had. "I showed the new owner my ideas for the ad campaign. He loved it. He's signed a nice contract with me. That client, along with the local jobs I've been getting, means I can stop traveling and stay in Kalispell full-time."

Jane lifted her hair off her neck again. "I'm glad for you, Nick."

He grinned and saw her swallow hard, feeling the tug of their attraction. "I've never given myself a chance to have any long-term relationship with a woman, Jane, but I do want that. I want to get married, like Quint. I want to have kids one day. Sooner, rather than later."

Jane's eyes widened, and he'd swear he spied a twinge of jealousy in their depths. "Then you have someone in mind already?"

Nick shook his head. "Nope, but I have a list."

"Of potential candidates?" Her expression said he was the same devil she'd always thought him.

"Don't worry. If I did, your name wouldn't be on it."

"I'm not worried."

He laughed. "It's a list of things I don't want in potential wife candidates. For instance, I won't be dating anyone with career plans that will take her out of the state, or out of the country."

"Like me," she said, obviously, finally getting it.

"Yes." *Even though I'd like nothing as much as stripping you naked right now and making you spend the night screaming my name in ecstasy.* "You intend to go to school, live, and work in France one day. And I'm happy for you. But I don't want to repeat my dad's life. I want to find someone, fall in love, marry, and then have children. No surprises."

Jane heaved a sigh. "And I don't want children."

"Exactly." But Nick didn't understand why her words made his heart feel so heavy.

Chapter Ten

An instrumental rendition of a country-western classic drifted through the kitchen of Big Sky Pie, the music a soft, nerve-soothing melody. The air held the fragrant scent of fresh-baked blueberry tarts. None of it calmed Jane's nerves. Three weeks had passed since she and the Tazmanian Devil had danced the mattress mambo, two weeks since they'd agreed to be adults about it and keep their hands off each other. It was what she wanted; it was what Nick wanted. There was no future for them together, and if they tried for one, it might end up with neither obtaining their personal goals.

So why couldn't she let it go?

It was like she'd been told to think about anything except chocolate, and then all she could think about was chocolate...until it became a craving. A craving for Nick. He chose that moment to turn his dreamy brown eyes toward her as if she'd spoken her thoughts aloud, as if he were taunting her. He glanced away quickly, but she thought she'd spied a flash of longing there. Probably not. Wishful thinking. He was already pursuing other women for possible fiancée prospects.

She'd overheard Andrea telling BiBi earlier that day that she'd set him up with a couple of her girlfriends on blind dates during the past two weeks, and the girlfriends reported back that they were smitten. BiBi's face went so red that Jane thought she might stroke out at the news. But she was taking advantage of her time with Nick now, batting her lashes, accidentally brushing up against him as they worked on tweaking the final ads for the grand opening. Jane pretended not to notice, tried not to care, but her temper slow-boiled like the blueberry filling she was stirring.

It wasn't as if Nick had totally ignored her. He'd interviewed her, photographed her making pies, and written a blog post or two featuring her in one way or the other. And she had to admit, the photographs he'd done were flattering, even if she was uncomfortable about everyone with Internet service being able to view them.

"Dad tells me that you've been helping Rebel with the wedding preparations, Jane," Nick said, leaning over her shoulder to see what she was doing.

Jane startled, nearly tipping the steaming pot. She swallowed, then spun to find his dimples on full display and swallowed again. "We ordered the flowers from Dean and Betty's shop, chose the reception hall, and I hear you're doing the invitations."

"I am."

God, he smelled good, better than the sugary-berry scent permeating the room. "Big Sky Pie is doing the pies for the reception."

"That's great."

It would be, Jane thought, but she hadn't been sleeping well, and to make matters worse, the past couple of days she had awakened feeling queasy. The last thing she needed was to come down with the flu. "We're going to look at gowns after I get off work today."

"Aren't you glad we decided to give them our blessings?" he whispered, close to her ear. Her skin rippled with sensuous goose bumps. "Dad seems on top of the world."

"I am glad," Jane said. She had to admit that her mother had never seemed this happy in any of her previous engagements. And Jane had never felt more miserable. She'd had her hands in so many blueberries this month that the tips of her fingers had taken on a bluish, frostbitten hue. Every time she noticed, she reminded herself that her hands weren't numb or frozen. It was her heart that had taken the hit.

"It's soooo romantic," BiBi butted in, obviously not liking it that Nick's attention was no longer on her. She hugged herself and sighed. "Rekindling a love that never really died."

Or trying to kill the embers of a love that had just begun to burn? Damn it. Why did she have to miss their bantering, and his dimples, and his kisses? Jane pulled the blueberry mixture from the stove and poured it into the waiting pie shells, then began layering on the lattice crusts. "BiBi, could you rinse out the pan I was just using?"

"Sure." BiBi smiled cheerily as though this were her favorite chore, the grin and good attitude meant to impress Nick. But Nick was packing up his laptop and answering his cell, nodding good-bye, and talking into the phone as he left the pie shop through the back door.

Jane watched him go, then ran to the bathroom and threw up.

* * *

The display windows of LaVina's Bridal Boutique faced Front Street. The mannequins wore lace and satin, and the air smelled like rose petal incense with an underlying hint of old building. Rebel introduced herself to LaVina and explained that she was relocating her Los Angeles–based wedding planning business to Kalispell. They exchanged cards as Jane looked around.

The walls were exposed brick, the floor washed concrete. Myriad wedding gowns crowded a couple of stand-alone brass clothing racks, while bridesmaid and prom dresses were deeper into the room, a rainbow hue of organza and taffeta. Veils occupied an antique wardrobe, and bejeweled headpieces were showcased in the glass-fronted counter. A couple of plants, a seating area, and a huge mirror added warmth and charm.

The dressing rooms were at the back of the store and were large, with three-way mirrors, love-seat-sized benches, and privacy doors. Rebel told LaVina what she had in mind for herself and for Jane, then dresses were pulled from the racks for consideration. Jane watched her mother as though seeing her for the first time, not as the teenager whose mom was behaving erratically and needed protection from herself, but woman to woman. There was a glow about her that came from within. Her eyes seemed to sparkle like diamond-cut ambers, her dark hair glistening like a sateen sheet, her coloring the perfect flush of healthiness. Happiness. *If this is what being in love does for a woman, why have I decided it's not for me?*

LaVina carried the selection of gowns to one of the four-by-four cubicles, and then Jane and her mother were alone. The maid of honor would wear aquamarine, but the choices did not inspire Jane to try them on. Despite not feeling well the past two weeks and eating less than usual, she seemed to have put on some weight, especially in her bust, and since she and her mother never agreed about what looked best on her...well, the situation could get uncomfortable.

Her mother gestured toward the wedding gowns. "Which one do you like best, Jane? Which should I try on first?"

She'd worn so many gowns throughout her life, in beauty pageants and six other weddings, each more beautiful than the last. It was a choice Jane could not make for her. "Well, what do you think?"

"Nothing pageant-y." They burst out laughing. Then Mom said, "Here, unzip me and I'll try the tea-length lace one." It was an off-the-shoulder style, in an ecru shade that would be gorgeous with her coloring. Rebel stepped out of her dress and stood there in a slip and heels, examining the gown in question.

"Mom, did you love Dad when you married him?" Jane blurted out, not meaning to ask but unable to stop herself.

Her mother went pale. Jane sank onto the stool. Rebel's shocked expression reflected again and again in the three-way mirror like a series of endless images, but lasted only for a couple of seconds as her natural self-possession kicked in. Grace under fire, always. "Why would you ask that, Janey? Of course I loved your daddy."

"As much as you loved Romeo?" *I never got over him.*

She hesitated, not putting on the dress, but holding it against her chest, considering the question before saying, "Your daddy was my first love, my teenage love. Those are always very special."

Something Gram Wilson had said popped into Jane's mind. "The other day I realized I know very little about your and dad's wedding and marriage. Did you marry him after you won the title of Miss Montana?" Beauty pageant winners had myriad obligations that extended beyond the title contest and often entailed yearlong contracts full of speaking engagements and running for Miss America. Jane frowned, realizing she'd never heard a whisper of her mother doing anything like that. *Wannabe beauty contestant*, Gram had called her. "Did you have to give up the title and the crown when you wed?"

Rebel folded the dress over her arm, sank to the bench seat next to Jane, and took hold of her daughter's hand. "I guess you're old enough and wise enough to handle how imperfect your mother is, but first you'll need a little background on my childhood. My mother began entering me in beauty contests when I was two or three years old. Mother, a former Miss America runner-up, wanted me to do what she'd failed to do—win that coveted title. That meant getting started earlier than she had. My childhood was a study in building my stage presence. My days consisted of poise classes, singing and dance lessons, costume fittings, and homeschooling."

Images came to Jane of her mother as a little girl competing in junior beauty pageants. In fact, she didn't recall any photos she'd seen of her mother as a child where she wasn't in pageant mode. None without big hair and Hollywood makeup, none in play clothes or ponytails, none with a dirty face and innocent eyes. "It must have been awful for you."

"I didn't know anything else."

"Didn't Poppy ever stand up for you?"

"Daddy adored Mother. He went along with anything she asked of him. We both did. If you'd known her, you might be able to understand that. She was dynamic, mesmerizing, as lovely as an angel, and when she wanted something, everyone seemed eager to comply. I can't explain it."

Jane wasn't sure she would have liked her maternal grandmother, given she'd treated her own daughter so badly. No wonder Rebel always craved attention. It was how she'd defined herself from her earliest years until today. Pity and new understanding twined through Jane's heart. She squeezed her mother's hand.

Rebel said, "I won a lot of small contests and big trophies as a child and into my early teens. And then I was up for the Miss Montana pageant, the last step to the big prize. All of Mother's hard work was about to pay off, or so she was convinced. She drove to Spokane to purchase some evening gowns for me." Rebel's eyes glazed as if she were looking back on something long ago, something excruciating. "She never made it home. A semi-truck collided with her compact on I-90, killing her instantly."

Jane rubbed her mother's arm gently, and Rebel gave her a bittersweet smile. "I fell apart. I couldn't stop crying. If she hadn't gone to Spokane for gowns for me, she'd still be alive. Your daddy was there, trying his best to console me, and I clung to him, the only thing keeping me from drowning in sorrow and guilt. As far as I was concerned, my life was over. I had nothing to live for. I couldn't go on. Not without Mother."

"How old were you?"

"Sixteen, almost seventeen."

Jane was still confused about her parents' marriage. "Daddy gave you the courage and strength to go ahead and enter and win the contest?"

"Not exactly." Rebel stared at their entwined fingers for a long moment, holding impossibly tighter as though she might lose Jane if she loosened her grip. "I mean, that's what we lead you to believe, but, well, I—I discovered I was going to have a baby."

The admission galvanized Jane. She whispered, "Me?"

"Yes. At first, I was frantic. I had no one to turn to. No one I could tell. Except Eddie. He was as overwhelmed as me, but he kept insisting we marry immediately. I wasn't sure. When I finally told my father, he wanted me to have a secret abortion." She hugged Jane. "Don't judge Poppy too harshly, sweetheart. He was a mess back then, too. He didn't think Eddie was good enough for me, and he couldn't bear losing Mother as well as her dream for me."

Jane felt blindsided. So this was why her mother had always told her to keep her eye on the prize, to protect herself against the pitfalls of sex. *She gave me every chance to make my own destiny, the very thing she had been denied her whole life.* It explained so much that Jane had never understood.

Rebel sighed. "Of course, I couldn't give up my child, and once Dad came to his senses, he felt the same. After we married, Eddie and I lived with him. Your dad finished high school and graduated with his class and worked nights and weekends at Wilson's Auto Barn. I got a GED from night school, and took some junior college courses in business management, and looked after you during the daytime."

"Until Romeo came along." And there it was, the resentment Jane couldn't quite shake, slipping out of her mouth like an accusation. Always under the surface, waiting to reach out and tear down any possibility that she would ever care for Nick's dad.

"What?" Rebel's brows knit together. "Heaven's no. I didn't meet Romeo until after the divorce."

Jane was sure this was wrong. Her mother was confused as to the dates and times of past events. Especially this past event. This life-altering event. "No."

"Yes." Rebel's expression shifted to that of a sudden revelation. "Is that what you've always thought? Is that why you don't like Romeo?"

Guilty as charged. "Well, uh, maybe..."

"Oh, my God." Rebel looked as though she might choke. "This is incredible. Romeo didn't break up my marriage to your daddy. Over the nine or so years we were husband and wife, the teenage infatuation that Eddie and I started out with ran its course and died. We were both miserable. Ending the marriage was a relief, and I had no intention of ever getting married again. I decided I needed money to continue college courses and find out what I did want to do. So I got a job as a bartender in a pretty lively bar, working nights so that I was home with you during the day, and Poppy could babysit in the evenings."

Mom stood, shook out the tea-length lace dress and stepped into it. As Jane zipped it for her, Rebel said over her shoulder, "Every night, good-looking, randy cowboys would try some lame pickup line or other on me. I got pretty great at dodging their clumsy advances. Then one night Romeo came in. The place was packed, and he brought his date to sit at the bar. He was about the most handsome man I'd ever seen, but it was not love at first sight."

Jane stepped back so her mother could see herself in the mirror. "What do you think?"

The dress hugged her mother's lean curves like it was made for her. "It's beautiful, but it looks more mother of the bride than bride."

"Agreed. Unzip, please." As Rebel stepped out of the dress and hung it on the hanger, she continued, "Romeo's date seemed to share my opinion of him. She seemed enthralled, but he looked as if he hoped someone would kidnap her. When she went to the ladies' room, I couldn't help myself. I asked him if he was on a blind date. He asked how I knew. We laughed. Then the date returned, and I didn't think any more about it. Until he showed up the next night, and the night after that. Alone."

Rebel chose a mermaid, floor-length style to try on next, and Jane helped secure the corseted back, then stepped back to assess the result while her mother turned in the mirror. "He sat at the bar, and whenever I had a few minutes, I would chat with him. We were both single parents, and from the way he spoke about Nick, I could tell that he loved his son as much as I loved you. So one night, about a month later, I broke down and went to a very early breakfast with him. We ended up talking until dawn."

The twinkle was back in her mother's eyes as she recalled the night. "What did Poppy say when you finally got home?"

"He said I needed to call next time I planned to be home that early." Mom made a face. "I don't think I like this see-through midriff. It's definitely sexy, but not my taste."

LaVina knocked at the door and asked how they were doing. They handed her the rejected dresses, and she appeared a moment later with another dress in hand. "I didn't show you this one because it's a larger size than you wear, Ms. Scott, but it's a Vera Wang, and it can be altered to fit if you like it."

"Okay, I'll try it." Rebel took the dress and shut the door. "What do you think, Jane? I like that it's not too full, and is a bit curve-hugging. Though I must say, this creamy, off-white color would be gorgeous with your complexion, sweetheart."

"Yes, but I'm not getting married, Mother." Not ever. *That's what I told Nick, and now he's speed-dating in order to find a bride.* The thought made her queasy again. Maybe she didn't have the flu after all. Maybe she was just sick about Nick.

"I hope one day, Jane, that you find your someone and feel the same kind of connection I felt after that night talking with Romeo. It was as if I'd found a part of myself, a part I hadn't even realized was missing. If that makes sense. I don't know, I can't explain it, but you know it when it happens."

The queasiness shifted, and light-headedness took its place. Jane sat back down on the bench. "Then why did you and Romeo get divorced?"

"Let's not talk about that." Rebel pulled up the

Vera Wang dress and appraised her image in the mirror. "I'm not sure about this one. I think it's a bit young for me."

"Here, darling, you try this one on." She handed Jane an aqua sheath.

Jane pulled the dress over her head and let it drop into place, then studied the effect in the mirror. The color did marvelous things for her skin and eyes, but the deep vee neckline and midcalf length were too mature. "This would look better on you."

"And this would look better on you. Too bad you're not the one getting married."

"Never." Jane blanched. She wanted to switch the subject, but how could she not think about romance in a bridal shop? And who better to answer her questions than her mother? She took a bracing breath and asked, "Mom, how do you know whether your feelings for a man are love or lust?"

Her mother's brows lifted, and she eyed Jane curiously. "Oh. So there is a man in your life. I rather suspected there might be. Who is he?"

Jane waved a dismissive hand. "I wouldn't say he's in my life the way you mean, but maybe I'd like him to be...for a while. The thing is, though, I don't want to fall in love, and I'm afraid, if I encourage what we're feeling, that might be the outcome."

"Love will always find a way, even if you shove it away and deny its existence. And you'll be miserable if you do. Been there, done that."

That was not the answer she wanted to hear. She took

off the aqua dress and reached for the next one, a fluffy chiffon number more appropriate for a junior prom than a maid of honor. "This looks like I'm wearing a pouf sponge."

"It does," Rebel said, bursting out laughing. She'd switched to a simple brocade dress with pockets that was more what Jane thought she should choose, but neither of them were moved to happy tears over it.

Jane removed the chiffon number and sank onto the bench again. "Mom, why did you and Romeo get divorced?"

"It's getting late," she said, stepping out of the dress and reaching for the skirt and top she'd worn into the store. "And I'm not finding anything. I guess the problem is, I've had too many weddings and too many gowns. I want something different, and none of these are different enough."

"I want to know," Jane persisted, gathering her own clothes and dressing.

"What did I tell you the last time you asked that?" Rebel hung up the brocade, her back to Jane.

"Money arguments."

"Well, there you go."

"I didn't believe it then, and now I really don't believe it."

"Well, then believe what you will. It's enough to know that we found each other again, and everything is different this time around."

Different how? Jane had to know the truth. "Vicky said that Nick and I came between you. That we were so awful—Nick to you, and me to Romeo—that we drove a wedge between you two. Did we?"

Rebel blanched. "Vicky Wilson should keep her mouth shut."

"Is it true?"

"It's true that you and Nick were both miserable, but what does that matter now? You and Nick are getting along great, and Romeo and I have never been happier. So instead of ancient history, why don't we direct our energies to your new romantic prospect?"

The idea of that brought the return of Jane's light-headedness and nausea.

* * *

Nick welcomed Quint McCoy and Wade Reynolds into the loft for their weekly bull session. He hadn't seen either of them for two weeks thanks to the Vegas trip with his dad.

Quint set a pie on the middle of the conference table. "Andrea tells me she fixed you up with a couple of her girlfriends on blind dates. I've met those women. A man could do a whole lot worse."

"Anything come of it?" Wade asked, bringing paper plates and silverware to the table. He'd stopped turning up his nose at their ritual of dessert before lunch for these get-togethers. The pies were that irresistible. "You get lucky?"

Nick laughed. "Hey, hey, let's keep it friendly here."

Quint and Wade exchanged glances. Wade said, "Oh yeah. He got lucky."

Quint teased, "And whoever she was, she got under his skin. Which one was it? Ashley with the big, beautiful booty?"

"Or Stephanie with the melon-sized—"

"None of your damned business."

Quint sighed. "Oh, Mr. Touchy. Yep, I'm thinking our guy isn't long for the single life, Reynolds. He's got all the symptoms of a bachelor going down for the count."

"You don't know how wrong you are," Nick said. He might've found the woman of his dreams, but loving her was a nightmare. She was everything he didn't want in a wife, and she didn't want a husband. He needed to forget her and move on. That was proving easier said than done. Andrea's friends were nice enough, but within two minutes of meeting each one, he knew the dates were going nowhere. He'd even done the unthinkable, spent the entire time he was with them talking about Jane. He'd known it was wrong after the first time, but that hadn't prevented him from giving it a repeat performance on the second date. There had to be some way to get Jane out of his system. Too bad sleeping with her again was out of the question.

"Have either of you ever been crazy about someone you couldn't have?" Nick asked.

Quint's head came up, and he ran his hand through his thick black hair, which seemed in perpetual need of a cut. "You mean like a married woman?"

Nick started to say, "No." But Jane was sort of married. To her career. "Something like that."

"Better not be my wife," Quint said, only half joking.

Nick shook his head. "Not Callee."

"As if she ever looks at anyone but you, McCoy," Wade said, bringing the coffeepot to the table and refilling everyone's drinks. "She's in permanent honeymoon mode."

Quint laughed. "And I intend to keep her that way."

"Then you'll always keep her," Wade said, a wistful look in his eyes for the wife he'd lost too soon in their young marriage.

"What's in the pie box?" Nick asked, lifting the lid, wishing now that he hadn't said anything to the guys. He wasn't ready to share the details of his screwed-up love life. This lingering infatuation would probably just run its course like all of his previous romantic entanglements.

"This is something different," Quint said, pulling out a creamy-looking pie. "The specialty at the shop this month is blueberry pie, but this is an old recipe that Jane said she got from her grandmother. Cottage cheese pie. Don't go turning up your nose, Reynolds. You like custard pie?"

"I do actually." Wade was eyeing the pie as if it were sour milk.

"Well, then you're gonna love this."

Nick frowned. Had he heard right? "Did you say Jane's grandmother made cottage cheese pie?"

Quint cut into the pie, then placed a slice on each plate, the aroma smelling of cinnamon and nutmeg. "That's what she said."

"My Granna Anna used to make this same pie. It was an old recipe she brought with her from Italy."

"Small world," Wade said.

Not so small, Nick thought, as he took a bite of his pie, stirring a long-forgotten memory. He and Jane were in Granna Anna's cozy kitchen on a cold winter night, enjoying a cup of cocoa and a piece of cottage cheese pie. It was one of the few joyful times he recalled during that year from hell. One of the first times Jane had seemed actually happy. He'd been surprised that she and his grandmother had taken to each other like water to flour, chattering about pies.

He was even more surprised now to realize his Granna Anna had done something she never did: shared a secret family recipe with Jane.

Chapter Eleven

❧

The day of the grand opening arrived with clear blue skies, temperatures forecasted for the low nineties, and a craziness Jane had never experienced. Balloons and banners decorated the outside of Big Sky Pie, and the parking lot held a couple of picnic tables for the pie-eating contest and another couple to handle the overflow of café customers. A hired DJ played current and classic country-western favorites, the music vibrating through the sunny morning.

Inside, the pie shop buzzed with last-minute preparations, the staff excited by the return of the proprietor, Molly McCoy. With her twinkling blue eyes, shocking red hair, and bubbly personality, Molly looked the epitome of good health. Her recovery made this celebration that much sweeter, Jane thought.

"Eight weeks and counting since the triple bypass," Molly said, seated at one of the stools around the work island. "My cardiologist calls mine a textbook recovery. He's only allowing me a couple of hours in the kitchen each day, though, so don't you worry, Jane, I won't be usurping your authority with the staff. I'm just another underling at the moment."

"I'm actually thrilled to have you here," Jane said, meaning it. Molly was famous for her blue ribbon pie skills. Jane didn't know how she was so lucky to have been selected to work in this pie shop—first to fill in for this woman, and now to work with her and learn from her. *My lucky stars must've been aligned over a field of four-leaf clovers that day.*

Jane wouldn't mind if she had been required to hand over the running of the kitchen. At least for a while. She was still battling exhaustion and queasiness—both coming on erratically for a few hours and then vanishing as though she had only imagined them. She kept thinking the virus, or whatever it was, would just go away, but it didn't, so she'd made an appointment with her doctor. Next Wednesday was the soonest he could fit her in. That was okay. She wasn't running a temperature; the only symptoms were the tiredness and nausea—which never got better or worse.

Probably an ulcer or some crazy sleep disorder.

At least the pie baking for the day was done. The aroma in the kitchen rivaled the sweetest flower Mother Nature could conjure, coming from the variety of blueberry delights—including tarts, turnovers, cream, and lattice-top pies—that occupied every counter, a bunch of stacking pie racks, and part of the Sub-Zero. And even the nausea hadn't killed her desire for the mouthwatering temptations.

"The *Flathead Beacon* and the *Daily Interlake* are both sending reporters," Nick said, walking in wearing jeans, cowboy boots, and a white dress shirt, which contrasted sexily with his olive skin. Jane's breath caught in her throat. *Wow, okay.* He was gorgeous—as sexy as any guy she'd ever met—and he did things to her insides that no other guy had done. But she didn't want a guy. She wanted a career. She didn't need a man. She needed her work. So why couldn't she stop thinking about the night they were together and yearning to be with the Devil again?

He turned his full attention on her, and she'd swear the light in his dark eyes seemed to shine a little brighter. Or maybe she just wished it did. "KCFW-9 is also sending a news crew. Jane, they're going to want to interview you and Molly."

"Well, hot damn. Quint promised I wouldn't be sorry if I hired you, Nick. And that son of mine knows what he's talking about." Molly clapped her hands in delight. "Imagine that. Missoula sending a TV news crew to cover our little grand opening. If that doesn't put us on the map, nothing will."

"Don't they want to speak to me about the pie-eating contest, Nick?" BiBi looked like a deflated balloon. Jane knew she wanted her father to see that her contribution to the grand opening was considered a big deal and that meant she had to get a mention in the papers or a sound bite on TV.

"BiBi should definitely get some portion of the media coverage," Jane said. *She's welcome to all of mine.* "She's done so much work, it should be publically recognized."

"I'm sure everyone will be interviewed, but it's up to the press what sound bite or angle they'll decide to focus on," Nick said, working his dimples. "And I'm pushing for Molly and you. Plus, I'll be photographing everything I can for the blog and updates on the event at the website."

"We'll do great, Jane," Molly said. "How soon will they be arriving, Nick?"

Nick checked his phone for the time. "Half an hour or so."

Andrea came in carrying a dress-sized box and plopped into an empty stool. She lifted the lid and pulled out some red-and-white-checkerboard fabric that turned out to be an apron. Big Sky Pie was embroidered across the top. "Callee had these made especially for the grand opening to identify pie shop employees to the public. Everyone gets one."

She handed the first to BiBi. "A couple of hungry-looking guys are in the café wanting to sign up for the pie-eating contest. You better get in there."

"Oh," BiBi said, a hand going to her short hairdo, which was all spiked and sporty today. The apron made her look even cuter. BiBi gave Nick a hot glance as she started for the café. "You might want to get a photo of me signing up contestants, Nick."

Nick, who had been taking pictures of the baked

goodies spread out around the kitchen, stopped what he was doing and trailed after Jane's assistant, camera to his eye. Probably aimed at BiBi's tight little rear, Jane grumbled to herself, restraining the urge to toss a blueberry tart at his broad back.

"Are you feeling okay?" Molly asked. "You seem a little pale, dear."

Jane tried to laugh it off. "I'm always a little pale."

"Well, just the same, you've been on your feet for hours already. You should take a bit of a rest before the day begins to get away from us."

"Oh, I'm okay." But Molly was having none of Jane's protests. "Go get some coffee and sit out back for a few minutes. Go. Do it."

The noise level in the café greeted Jane as she entered from the kitchen. Customers were queued out the door. One queued to the counter, where Andrea and a temp, hired for the event, were selling pie by the slice. The DJ had cranked the music, giving the whole affair a party feeling. Jane smiled and nodded at a few of the customers that she recognized, squeezing through one line to get to the coffee station.

She heard her dad call, "Janey, over here, baby."

Eddie, Vicky, and Wilma Wilson were wedged into one of the booths, enjoying some blueberry pie à la mode and mugs of coffee. "We came to support you on your big day. Sit down and join us."

"I'd love to, Dad, but I'm working."

"Oh sure, baby, we understand." His face lit up with pride. "It's a great party you're throwing."

Jane didn't stop to tell him it wasn't her party. She wanted to get some coffee and take it to a place where she could sit and hear herself think. But another male voice called out to her, "Jane!"

The next second she was lifted off her feet as if she were a child and spun into Liam's arms. "I see your knees are better, eh? I was wondering since you haven't called or come in for another training session. You have paid for them, you know, and the gym offers no refunds. I'd hate to see you lose that money."

Liam's icy blond hair flopped over his forehead, a deep contrast to a tan she suspected he'd gained in a tanning bed. He'd traded his gym gear for jeans and a muscle shirt, and he smelled of some musky aftershave. BiBi was looking Liam up and down as though he were a platter of a newly discovered, newly favorite dessert.

"Uh, Liam," she said, "we haven't finished filling out your contest application."

"Oh, sure, I'll be right there, eh?" He set Jane down, and that was when she saw Nick, camera at his eye, aimed at her. What the hell? If he was doing crowd shots for the website, this was one she didn't want to see there.

Liam caught her chin with one finger, drawing her attention from the Devil. She had to admit the former Canadian ski champion was definitely cover model material, with his broad shoulders, his lean-muscled body, and the cleft in his chin, but she didn't feel anything when he touched her. Nothing. What was the matter with her? If she had to have sexy fantasies about a man, why not this one?

"So, Jane," he said, "can I count on seeing you this week, then?"

The last thing Jane had time for at the moment was working out at the gym—especially when she might run into Nick there. Encountering him at work most days was hard enough. She hated lying to Liam, but heard herself say, "Of course. I'll call and set up an appointment."

His blindingly white teeth flashed in a snowy smile. "Great. I'll look forward to it, eh?"

He headed toward BiBi, and Jane proceeded to the coffee station. Nick appeared at her side as she stirred cream into her mug. "What did he want?"

She peered up at him, surprised by the inquiry, cautioning herself not to read more into it than curiosity. "I could tell you, but it's really no concern of yours, is it?"

"The intentions of potential suitors for the affections of my soon-to-be baby stepsister definitely fall into the realm of my concern."

Jane wasn't sure if she should be flattered, pleased, or angry. She'd been yearning for this exact kind of attention from him, but it wasn't in either of their best interests, and he knew it. His citrus scent wound into her nostrils and scrambled her better sense. She couldn't think when Nick stood this close. "Liam is not a potential anything. He's my personal trainer. Period."

"Nick! Oh, Nick!" BiBi called, waving her hand frantically as if she were on fire and Nick was the only one in the room who could work an extinguisher. Given the speed with which he responded, she wondered if her assistant had gotten her wish and was about to be Nick's next sexual conquest. The possibility sent a flash of sickening heat through Jane. But why? She didn't want Nick. He was free to date whomever he chose.

Growling at herself, she carried her coffee and her inappropriate, unrelenting jealousy outside for some sobering fresh air. It didn't help.

When Molly came to get her for their interview with the reporters, Jane was still feeling rocky. Shaky. Too much caffeine, probably, mixed with a ready jittery nerves that seemed to be keeping beat to the foot-stomping Blake Shelton melody generated from the other side of the building. She should have settled for a bottle of water instead of coffee. "I'd really rather BiBi sat in with you. She's dying for the media attention."

"Yes, but you're the one who makes these delicious pies, and that is, after all, the heart of this shop, now isn't it?"

How could Jane argue against that? Or argue with her boss? She couldn't. But when they strode into the café looking for the newspaper and TV reporters, they spied them around BiBi and a man with a gray streak in his dark hair and a commanding presence. He seemed vaguely familiar, but Jane couldn't place him.

"Who is that with BiBi?" she asked Andrea.

Molly gasped. "Why, it's Chopper Henderson. He used to be on the Food Network. For years."

"I remember him," Andrea said. "My mom used to watch him."

"He was a big deal, until he got into a war of egos

with one of the other chefs on that channel, and he used a sexual slur about the guy on a talk show. Huge scandal ensued, the whole country in an uproar, insisting the powers that be at the network fire him. Ruined his career."

"Does he live in Kalispell?" Jane asked.

"Yes," Molly answered absently. "But don't waste any pity on that one. He's a millionaire many times over, most of it made from his how-to tapes, cookware, kitchen gadgets, and cookbooks. He just misses the fame." She stopped, her mouth dropping open. "Andrea, why is Chopper talking to those reporters?"

"They were thrilled to discover his daughter works here and decided that would be a great angle for their news stories," Andrea said, adding as an aside to Jane, "Chopper is BiBi's father."

"Oh," Jane said. Understanding finally why BiBi wanted to achieve success without his name attached to it. It wasn't just to impress him, but to dissociate herself from his tainted reputation.

"Why, that wily old coyote," Molly huffed in outrage. "He's using my grand opening to get himself back into the limelight, and those lamebrained reporters are aiding and abetting. This has disaster written all over it. Where's Nick? Somebody find him quick."

Molly's coloring grew redder with every word, not a good sign in someone who had recently recovered from bypass surgery. Jane and Andrea escorted her back to the kitchen and onto a stool.

Andrea said, "You wait here. I'll find Nick and make sure he sends Chopper packing. But I'm sure you realize, Molly, that the reporters and the TV crew will take way more photos and notes than they will or can use. And we have zero input into what makes it into the articles or sound bites. The result might not be what you're hoping for."

"Maybe not, but at least it should be about Big Sky Pie and not about whatever bill of goods Chopper Henderson is selling. He had his fifteen minutes of fame."

Nick was found, and he and Molly went to chat with the reporters and divert their focus back to the pie shop. The TV crew hadn't arrived yet. Andrea gave the counter girl some pies to restock the display cases in the café, and Jane sat at the work island with a drink of water, glad for a moment alone. A moment was all she had.

BiBi came into the kitchen with murder in her eyes. Although she suspected what it was about, Jane asked, "Something wrong?"

"Can you believe that?" BiBi's hands were gesturing faster than someone fluent in sign language. "I've worked my butt off getting this pie-eating contest pulled together, not to mention making the pies for it and helping Callee and Nick with the advertising, and everyone wants to steal my thunder. Including my own dad."

"Oh? You didn't look like you minded."

She sighed. "It's my dad. What am I supposed to do? I couldn't tell him to buzz off, though I wanted to. I just thought he'd, you know, know better."

"Well, that's the thing about our folks. They make mistakes."

BiBi was anything but placated. She wanted to be the big cheese of the grand opening, a ridiculous expectation. Today wasn't her day. It was Molly McCoy's. But Jane did feel bad for her. "Did your dad teach you your pastry skills?"

"He didn't teach me anything, though I have asked him since I was little. He would just shoo me out of the kitchen, telling me I was too young. I could get hurt. I might cut myself. Burn myself. Well, I taught myself how to make pies." BiBi paced, hands flapping. "But just now, he implied to those reporters that he'd taught me everything I knew. That I was a chip off the Chopper block, his little joke."

"I'm sorry."

She wiped a tear away. "Didn't it occur to him that he was stealing my moment? My chance to show him that I can make it in his profession without using his former professional status to give me a leg up?"

"Sometimes dads aren't the most sensitive to our needs."

But BiBi knew Jane's dad was not like hers because Jane had told her how he always supported her no matter what. BiBi snapped, "You don't have a clue. No one ever gives me a chance to prove what I can do. No one seems to appreciate my talents. Especially my dad. It's always all about him."

"He was a star for many years. I would imagine that being the center of attention is a difficult thing to give up."

"I'm sure you'll find out just how hard someday, but the way things are going for me, I'll never get that chance," BiBi railed. "God, I'm such an idiot. Was it always this way? Did I just refuse to see it? Was I too blinded by hero worship to see my dad for who he really is?"

She wasn't asking Jane; she was asking herself. Jane took a sip of water, striving to come up with some way to cheer her up. "When does the pie-eating contest start?"

"In about half an hour."

"Do you have a lot of contestants?"

"More than I figured on. Three picnic tables' worth. Good thing I made an extra dozen pies."

"You're going to rock the event." Jane smiled encouragement. "Don't let what's happened ruin anything for you. You're too much like that person on the daughters with rich fathers show."

"Huh?"

"You know, Ariel Magnus what's her name from your favorite reality show...about the Hollywood millionaires' daughters."

"Ariel is like you, not me." BiBi let loose a not-nice laugh. "I'm more like Valentine Ricci."

The way she said this sent a shiver down Jane's spine. "Who's that?"

"The mean girl."

Jane took a sip of water, wanting to end the conversation. The crowd noise and the music seemed to be getting louder and louder, pulsing through the pie shop as though the walls were thumping. She felt an ache start at her temples. She needed time to compose her thoughts before anyone interviewed her. Maybe she could escape to the mall.

"Oh, hey, I think the TV crew just arrived." BiBi jumped up and peered out the back windows. "Yep, that's them. How do I look?"

"Great."

"You do, too." She started toward the café. "Are you coming?"

"I, ah, Andrea needed some whipped cream. There's some in the storeroom refrigerator." Jane spun away and ducked into the back hallway that led to the cold room. The space was large and filled with rows of shelving, reminding her of a library, but with fresh fruits and canned goods and extra pie-making supplies instead of books. There was also a second Sub-Zero as well as another freezer.

Andrea hadn't really asked for more whipped cream, but Jane figured she'd better bring some with her just in case BiBi was still in the kitchen when she returned. Although she hoped her assistant would be gone by then. The chill air brushed her bare arms as she stepped deep into the room and started walking to the Sub-Zero. A creak sounded behind her. She spun to see the door closing.

Jane swore. The music and crowd noise was barely discernible thanks to triple insulated walls, but it was too cold to be in here for more than a couple of minutes in a sleeveless sundress, apron, and sandals. She grabbed a container of Reddi-wip from the Sub-Zero and hurried to the door. The knob wouldn't turn. She tried again. It was locked. Was this a joke? Recalling BiBi's mean girl comment, she decided it might not be. She banged on the door. "This isn't funny, BiBi. Let me out! BiBi!"

BiBi didn't answer. And Jane realized that no one would hear her over the music and voices or through the soundproof walls. It wasn't so cold she would freeze to death. It wasn't so airtight she'd lose oxygen, but she was stuck here until someone realized she was missing or came looking for her. She gave the door a couple of good whacks, then hugged herself against the cold as a tear rolled down her cheek.

She turned back toward the room and saw the Devil standing there, looking as annoyed as she felt. Her heart almost stopped. "Why didn't you tell me you were here?"

"I didn't want to startle you."

"Too late." Her heart was thudding beneath her hand pressed to her chest.

He seemed to notice the tears on her cheeks. He set his camera equipment on a shelf and started toward her. "Ah, don't cry, Pain. I won't let anything happen to you."

"Did you lock this door?"

"Me? Hell no. I was near the back wall photographing some fresh strawberry and cherry flats for the blog."

"Swear on your father's life?"

He looked as though her request was ludicrous. "Seriously, why would I lock us in here? Oh my God, you're shivering." Nick tugged off his white dress shirt and draped it over her bare shoulders.

His body heat lingered in the shirt, along with his citrusy scent. Jane hugged the shirt to her, her gaze fixed on his bare chest. She shivered. Nick seemed to mistake it for the cold. She let him reach for her, pull her into his arms, and dry her tears. The yearning she couldn't deny filled her so full that she thought she'd explode.

"Oh, God, Jane, don't look at me like that... please...or I won't be responsible—" He swallowed hard and tried to release her, but her mouth found its way to his...

Chapter Twelve

⁓

Is like knowing what pie is-a your favorite, Nicola. The taste, she lingers on-a your tongue long after the last little bite is-a gone, and you can no wait until you have-a some more. Then-a you know. Is the one."

And Jane was the taste he'd longed for, the one he couldn't get over. His heart's favorite flavor. His body knew the second her lips met his, the kiss speaking to some primal part of his being, telling him that this was *the* woman. His woman. His mate.

Music seemed to surround them, not the country beat the DJ was playing, but violins and harps, a love song as enchanting as the ages. Nick felt swept up in it. Desire flared through him, a wildfire, sizzling his blood, burning every thought that wasn't Jane from his mind. He swept her to him, his arms filled with her wonderful curves, his body instantly hard and thrumming, his breath coming quick and sharp, like his heartbeat.

He reached into her hair, and soon, loosened pins fell through his fingers, the French braid unknotted, and Jane's satin curls bounced free, smelling like lilacs after a spring rain. The chill in the room stole across his naked back like a cool breeze, and Nick pulled Jane closer, fearing that she might be too cold still, but everywhere he touched felt toasty, inviting him to touch more.

He couldn't resist. His hand slid beneath her filmy dress and up her sleek legs to snag on a flimsy bit of silkiness, his fingers moving it aside to find the nest of dense, damp curls, finding the center of her passion. She reacted with a soft, sweet squeal...his name on her lips spiking his need higher, her hands on his back erasing all memory of chilly air. He deepened their kiss, pleasuring her again, finding his enjoyment linked with hers. The greater her bliss, the greater his.

Her small hands moved to stroke his chest, and then his stomach, and finally reached the top of his jeans. She fumbled with the button at his waist for a few seconds, until he freed it for her, but then he let her undo the zipper, let her push his jeans down his legs, let her find her way at her own speed, the journey a trail of wet kisses and joyous torture.

He let her do what she would to him until he could stand it no longer, then he pulled her to him, kissing her again and again, and lifted up and up. She locked her legs around his hips and lowered herself onto him as he pushed inside her, deep and quick, deep and quick. As he gazed into her eyes, the room disappeared, blue sky abounding as they shot toward the clouds, each rush higher and faster than the last. He felt her body spasm, heard her murmur his name, and his own climax slammed into him like a velvet fist.

They clung together, their twined breaths the only sound in the room as they floated gently back to earth. To reality. Jane made no move to disentangle herself from him, but he held her as tightly as before, savoring the feel of her in his arms, the weight of her legs around his hips. She felt like home, safe, the one place he always wanted to be. And he knew that he had fallen in love with her. He hadn't meant to. She wouldn't want to hear it, but it was the sad, sorry truth.

"Oh, Nick," Jane said, laying her head on his shoulder. "I'm so confused. I don't want to fall for you. I don't want you to fall for me. So what's going on? Why am I miserable at the thought of you dating other women? Why can't I think of anything else but doing what we just did?"

Call it being a guy, call it anything you want, but her confession revived his libido faster than any little blue pill might have. He grinned at Jane. "You want to do it again?"

A look of complete misery played across her face. "Oh, God, yes. Do you?"

He laughed and kissed her, and a moment later, the heat raged hotter than the first time.

Later, Nick thought he might collapse onto the floor and dissolve into a pool of afterglow. His limbs were wobbly, his body sated, his face locked in a silly grin.

"Jane, you are a pain, a wonderful, glorious, delicious pain."

Jane seemed less joyous than he. She covered her lush body with her long skirt, adjusted her apron, and began gathering the pins he'd torn from her hair. He watched as she tried to blindly refix the French braid. "Can you do that without a mirror?"

She blew out a breath and lowered her hands. "Not really. I just didn't want whoever comes to free us noticing my disheveled appearance and jumping to the wrong conclusions."

"Or to right ones." He smirked.

"I wonder when someone will notice we're missing and come looking for us..."

"Are you cold?" he asked. Now that they were no longer generating body heat, the temperature in the room seemed to have dipped ten more degrees. It had probably not changed, but his internal register had.

"Yes. I am cold," she said, rubbing her arms.

"Well, I could cuddle you some more. Or I could call Quint to come rescue us."

She stopped moving and stared at him wide-eyed. "You have your phone?"

"Sure."

"Why didn't you say so right off?"

"Well, if you recall..."

She blushed. She did recall. "What are we going to do, Nick? About us? You're looking for a serious relationship that will lead to marriage. I'm not the woman for you, no matter how this, this physical attraction, begs to disagree, and it would be pure selfishness to keep you from finding the right person."

"You have my permission to be as selfish as you want..." He reached for her, but she stepped back, hugging herself.

"I'm serious, Nick." She pleaded with her eyes for his understanding.

Nick felt something crack inside his chest and realized it might be a fissure skating across his breaking heart. "You don't mean that."

"I do."

"You expect me to walk away as if this didn't happen?" Twice.

"No, no. It did happen. I'm not sorry that it did either. I'll remember it always."

"Always?" Nick shoved his arms into his shirt and began working the buttons. This wasn't the first time a woman had said this to him. He knew a kiss-off when he heard it. "So you want us to go back to acting like acquaintances?"

She nodded. "I guess."

Nick caught hold of her by the upper arms, firmly but gently bringing her up against him. "No. We tried that. It didn't work."

Sounding breathless, she said, "Then what can we do? Be friends with benefits?"

The suggestion coming from Jane was unexpected and laughable. Yet he wanted to say a resounding, "Hell yes! I'll take any bone you throw me." He stared at her mouth, that damned tempting mouth, and he knew if he was anywhere near her that he would always want to kiss her, always want to make love to her, and he wouldn't care who knew it. But in the end, she would go to France, and he would be hurt even worse than he was hurting now. For his own sake, he needed to make a clean break.

He released her to tuck his shirttail into his jeans. Damn it all. Why did relationships have to be so complicated? Why wasn't love enough? "I can't do friends with benefits, Jane. Not with you. It's all or nothing. So it better be nothing."

He pulled his phone out of his pocket and dialed Quint's number.

* * *

The second Quint unlocked the door, Jane headed straight for the bathroom. The mirror told the story of her every sin from tousled hair to lips still swollen from Nick's kisses to skin flushed with satisfaction. She set the hairpins on the counter and began fixing her French braid. Five minutes later, she emerged from the bathroom looking like her normal self, but feeling as if a stranger had invaded her body. Her mind. Who was this woman who couldn't stop longing for a man? Not her. Not Jane. Jane Wilson made goals and met them. She didn't take risks. She didn't make love to men in the cold room. Twice. That was so not her. This was Nick's fault. Somehow he'd bedeviled her.

Nick's parting words came back to her and, with

them, the return of her nausea. She'd hurt him. She hated herself for that, but she owed him honesty. If she'd done the right thing, why did it feel so wrong?

As she walked through the kitchen, the upbeat country music seemed to swirl through the rooms, encircle her, and pull her toward the source. Jane resisted, moving slowly. Someone had cleaned the counters and work island for the next day already, and the previously jam-packed racks were now empty. Molly would be pleased at the number of pies, tarts, and turnovers that they'd sold on this first day of the grand opening, and hopefully this would translate into a lot of future business.

The café was empty. Andrea and the temporary help stood in the doorway, facing the parking lot. The music stopped abruptly, and BiBi's voice boomed over a loudspeaker garnering cheers and hoots as she announced that she was ready to declare the winners of the pie-eating contest and hand out prizes. Jane strode up to Andrea in time to see Liam whirling BiBi around in a big bear hug. "Did Liam win?"

"Nope," Andrea said over her shoulder. "Came in third."

"Oh, who won?"

Andrea glanced at her as though taken aback. "Where were you that you don't know?"

"I, I wasn't feeling well."

"Again?"

Jane pressed her lips together and shrugged.

"Maybe you need to see a doctor. What if you're contagious and the whole town comes down with the same bug?"

A clammy chill swept through Jane. "Oh, God, what if I am?"

Andrea laughed. "If you were, I'm sure I would have been the first one to catch it. My boys are always gifting me with some germ or the other."

BiBi announced the second-place winner, a woman who couldn't weigh ninety pounds dripping wet. "Are you kidding me? How did she out eat Liam?"

"The contest was timed. Not how many pies you could eat in a given time, but who could eat a whole pie the fastest."

"Did anyone get sick?"

"A couple of the biggest guys," the temp said, laughing.

"And last, but not least, Big Sky Pie's grand opening, grand prize winner for the first annual pie-eating contest is Mr. Eddie Wilson of Wilson's Auto Barn."

Jane's mouth dropped open. "My dad won?"

"Yep."

He'd been eating pie and ice cream earlier. It was amazing that he hadn't gotten sick. "And nobody called 'fixed' on us?"

"There were a few grumbles, but he was a pie-eating Pac-Man. Came in a whole minute under everyone else."

Laughing, Jane watched her dad accept the trophy with the miniature baker holding a pie on top and the gift certificate for a free pie a week for six months. He did love pie, but he really should gift that certificate to someone without his connection to this establishment. As if he'd read her mind, he reached down to a young woman holding a baby, her husband beside her, arms full of a squirming two-year-old, and gave them the gift certificate. At their surprised, delighted, uncertain expressions, he explained to them and the crowd that his daughter, Jane, was one of the pastry chefs at Big Sky Pie, and he would not be deprived of his share of desserts.

The crowd cheered his generosity, and Jane felt a swell of love. "I need to go congratulate him." She squeezed past Andrea and the temp and moved through the crowd, noticing as she neared that her dad's shirt-front was smeared with blueberry juice. Vicky would probably have a fit when she saw it.

"Janey! How about your old man? Fastest eater in the state." He pulled her into a hug.

"We'll be buying a bottle of bromide on the way home," her grandmother said.

"That's a great trophy, Eddie," his wife said, not even glancing at his stained shirt, just sharing in the joy he was feeling over his victory.

"Congratulations, Eddie." Rebel seemed to appear out of nowhere.

Wilma went as still as a tree, Vicky paled, and Jane held her breath, praying her grandmother would not cause a scene.

Eddie's grin faltered for half a second, then widened, his gaze assessing her from head to toe. "Rebel, I heard you were in town. Getting married again, huh?"

"I am. For the last time."

Vicky went territorial and looped an arm through her husband's, and Gram mumbled under her breath, "Yeah, sure."

Jane caught her mother's arm, trying to haul her away before World War III broke out, but her mother resisted. "Wilma, look what teaching Jane to bake pies has led to. Thank you. I'm sure you're all as proud of our girl as I am."

It was the one thing none of them could dispute. How they felt about Jane. Jane glanced at BiBi, thought about her assistant's dreadful relationship with her father, and her anger toward BiBi for locking her in the freezer faded. Sometimes it was better to be grateful for your blessings than to seek revenge, especially for an act of petty jealousy.

"If someone doesn't take me home soon, I'm gonna collapse in this heat. Been on my feet too damned long." Gram stared pointedly at Eddie.

He took the hint, kissed Jane, nodded at Rebel, and hustled his wife and mother to his shiny new pickup truck.

Jane turned to her mother. "I'm so glad to see you."

"I couldn't miss your triumphant moment." The pride in her voice was genuine, and Jane knew she was right to choose her career over love and marriage. Those things were not for someone like her, but for someone like her mom. "Where's Romeo?"

"He's with the DJ, talking about booking him for our reception. He's quite good, you know. Turns out he's a friend of Nick's."

Jane's gaze skipped over the thinning crowd to where the DJ's stand was. She spied Romeo, and beside him... Nick. Her heart did a flip, and then a flop. He'd managed to do what nothing else and no one else in her life had done. Slain the bullies that lived in her mind. Made her feel beautiful despite the extra pounds, despite her flaws. He'd given her a new confidence that would see her through her goals, goals that didn't match his. The gift she owed him in return was to walk away.

"We've been looking for you and Nick for a couple of hours," Mom said. "So where were you two hiding?"

Jane's face went hotter than a sunburn. But before she could answer, one of the TV people tapped her shoulder. "Are you the pastry chef who was locked in the cold room with Nick Taziano? I'd like to include the incident in our news clip."

"What?" Her mother's eyebrows almost reached into her scalp.

Jane tried to blow it off. "It was just an accident. Trust me. Nothing newsworthy went on."

"Are you sure?" Rebel whispered.

"Yes," Jane whispered back. "Nothing."

"Then why are you blushing like a rose?"

"Too much sun." Jane was not going to do any interview that involved talking about Nick and the cold room. She told the reporter that she needed to freshen up if she was going to be on TV, then Jane hurried into the café, through the kitchen, and out the back door. But she wasn't getting away that easy. Andrea was sitting in the employee area with her sons.

Andrea waved her over. "We're taking a rest from the mayhem. The boys had a little too much sugar. Lucas ate most of Logan's pie, but Logan ate all of Lucas's ice cream."

"It was good," Logan, the younger one, said, licking his lips.

"I like pie better than ice cream," Lucas said.

"Me too." Jane laughed, but she wasn't feeling much joy. The heartache of finally deciding she had to let go of Nick was sinking in full force, and with it came the return of her weariness. She was glad that Molly and Quint were going to handle any pies that might be needed for day two of the grand opening week. She'd been given the day off, and she intended to spend it in bed.

And she did. All day. She didn't answer the phone, didn't have visitors, just slept for the first time in weeks. But when she awoke, she was sad and resigned. She and Nick were over.

* * *

The next ten days passed as if she were an automaton, doing what she did best, ending each day tired and satisfied with the work. Nick hadn't been to the pie shop since the first day of the grand opening. Jane hated not seeing him, but knew she'd done the right thing. If not for herself, for him. Still, her nights were lonely, and the troubling nausea was lingering in the mornings.

BiBi had finally apologized for locking her in the

cold room, although she didn't look apologetic. "I admit it. I wanted to feel special, to be appreciated for all the work I'd done, but everyone kept focusing on you. Even Nick. Okay, so I was jealous. I'm sorry. I really didn't mean to be a mean girl."

Jane wasn't holding a grudge, but she didn't want her assistant to think she could pull something like that again without consequences. "Just don't do it again."

"Yeah, well, it backfired on me anyway, since I locked Nick in there with you." Her gaze went curious. "Anything you want to share about that?"

"I hear you have a date with Liam coming up?" Jane said, changing the subject.

BiBi tipped her head and grinned. "He's really built."

"Yes, he is," Jane agreed, then went back to rolling pie dough.

Around ten that morning, she encountered Andrea outside enjoying an espresso at the employees' table. The sky was a solid mass of baby blue, the air comfortably warm and so sweet it could make you high. Jane sat, feeling the weariness grab hold of her. Andrea studied her a moment, and then said, "Have you been to your doctor's yet?"

"Tomorrow."

"Good." Andrea took a sip of her drink, then said, "I know it's none of my business, and if I'm being too personal, you can tell me to buzz off, but could you possibly be pregnant?"

The question startled Jane. She hadn't thought of that, and now that it was in her head, her first impulse was to flat out deny it. "Oh, God, I hope not. I don't want kids. Not now. Not ever."

"I know, but you sure have a lot of the same symptoms I went through."

"No. I'm positive." But was she? She dug her cell phone from the pocket of her apron and checked the calendar. Her heart sank. "I missed my last period...by three weeks."

"It could be stress. You've been under a lot of pressure," Andrea said.

That was true. "And I've never been particularly regular."

By the time she left work, she'd convinced herself, and Andrea, that it wasn't possible. But on the way home, she bought a pregnancy test.

Chapter Thirteen

⁓

This is the best bachelor party I've ever had." Nick's dad held up a beer bottle in a salute from his position at the helm of the thirty-five-foot boat Nick had rented for the occasion. Flathead Lake was approximately twenty-seven miles long, fifteen miles wide, and as deep as three hundred seventy feet in some places. He'd driven the boat out into one of the areas considered by locals to be ideal for fishing and cut the engine. There wasn't a whisper of wind, the water dark and smooth as acrylic.

"Far as I know, it's the only bachelor party you've ever had," Nick said from the captain's chair. He couldn't have asked for a better day, the sky as blue as the berries in Jane's pies, the sun hot and high, the water cold and deep, and the trout and freshwater salmon eager to snap onto the bait.

"Thank you, son," Romeo said, then swallowed from the long-necked bottle and smacked his lips.

"Yeah," Quint said, baiting his hook. "Most guys would have thought strip club and lap dances."

"When you live in Vegas as many years as I did, T and A are old hat, McCoy," Romeo said. "But being out on a lake with a bunch of rowdy rednecks, fishing our asses off, smoking cigars, and bragging about the ones that got away, that's my idea of a celebration."

"Especially when the rainbow and kokanee are biting, like today," Wade Reynolds added, casting his line into the water, a cigar hanging from his mouth.

"Damn straight," Quint said, lifting his pole to reel in another fish. "Guess what's for dinner?"

Only Nick hadn't caught any fish or had any fun, although he'd put on the biggest sales pitch of his life convincing these guys—his two best pals and two of his dad's longtime friends who'd flown in from Vegas—otherwise.

Only Quint didn't seem to be buying his act. That was the trouble with friends who knew you too well. Quint came up to the bridge and sat in the seat opposite Nick, holding a beer bottle by the neck. He was quiet for a moment, then leveled his gaze on Nick. "You once told me I had the look of a man with female problems. Unless I'm mistaken, you're in that very position right now. Whoever she is, she's got your tail in a twist."

"Fuck you, McCoy," Nick said. His heart was a bleeding bruise in his chest, the pain and the source private. Not something he wanted to share even with his best friend. Not now, at least. Someone might overhear. It might ruin his dad's party.

"Wow, it's more serious that I suspected." Quint lifted his cowboy hat from his head, finger-combed his mop of black hair, and studied Nick with those bright blue laser beams he called eyes. They could probe a man to the core of the matter. Damn him.

Nick looked away and muttered, "She doesn't want to be in love."

"Love? Hmm. Definitely more serious than I was thinking. Are you in love?"

Nick stared at the fishing line on his pole, spotting the bait inches below the water's surface. He hadn't lowered the line enough to catch anything. "'Fraid so."

Quint drank from his beer, his hat brim low, his gaze pointed toward Romeo's two buddies on the bow of the boat. "You didn't say she didn't love you, only that she didn't want to be in love."

"Same fucking thing."

Quint glanced sideways at him. "Now there, my friend, you are wrong."

Nick scrubbed at his unshaved jaw, the stiff whiskers rough against his palm. "How do you figure that?"

"Well, she could be in love with you and refusing to acknowledge it, even to herself."

Nick sighed. "Even if she did feel that way, it won't change anything. She has career ambitions."

"Ambitions you aren't on board with?"

Nick thought about his mother. "That's right. I'm not."

"Why? Does she want to go to Vegas and strip for a living?"

"She wants to live in Europe for a few years."

"Whoa." Quint sat straighter and spread his arms wide. "Why would anyone want to leave Montana?"

"She wants to go to culinary school in France." The moment he said it, he knew that he'd said too much, that Quint would know who he was talking about.

He felt Quint's eyes boring holes into him. "Jane? You're in love with Jane?"

Nick said nothing. His grimace said it for him.

"Well, fuck me." Quint was grinning and nodding. "Yeah, I could see that."

"Will you stop enjoying my misery?"

"Like you stopped enjoying mine?"

"Yeah, well, you were being an ass. You made your own misery."

Quint looked sheepish. "True, but you're kind of doing the same, aren't you?"

"What?" Nick said. "Maybe you should lay off the beer."

Quint took another slug of his Bud Light. "Did Jane say she didn't love you?"

"No, but she didn't say she loved me either."

"Look, I know she has her eyes set on school in France at some point, but that's not for another year or two."

"She's afraid being married will end that dream."

"Would it? Would you be the kind of husband who couldn't put his wife's dream before his own?"

Nick thought about that. He didn't want Jane to lose her dream. It meant too much to her. When he'd set his sights on owning his own advertising business, the most important, influential person in his life then was his dad. Romeo hadn't stifled those dreams, but rather he'd encouraged Nick to follow his heart. Nick couldn't do less for the woman he loved. "I don't want to ever be the reason that Jane doesn't reach her goals."

"Last I heard, France has Wi-Fi. And the work you do is mostly by computer. Hell, you're not pinned to Montana or Kalispell. You could do what you do in Paris for a couple of years, with the occasional business trip to the States, if it meant being with the woman you love. It's not the location that counts when you've found the love of your life."

As Quint's words sank in, the pain in Nick's chest eased, and Nick started to grin. "Don't believe all the rumors going around about you, McCoy. You're not such a dumb shit."

"Hey, somebody toss up a couple of beers. The host has finally decided to join the party." He cranked up the CD player on a favorite old Garth Brooks song about friends in low places. It seemed apropos. "Now let's catch some fish."

* * *

The windows of Jane's apartment were open to the sunny afternoon, birds singing outside and a whirring fan to stir the hot air. She had changed from work attire to shorts, a tank top, and flip-flops. Her mother showed up in a breezy sundress, as tanned and lovely as a beach goddess.

Jane placed the plastic sandwich bag on the island. A whole day had passed, and yet the news hadn't fully sunk in. Her mother bent toward the object inside, gasped, then turned to Jane with eyes wide and her mouth open. "Is this what I think it is?"

"Yes," Jane's voice squeaked out. When her mother found herself in this situation, she'd had no one turn to and very little recourse. Jane was older, luckier. Times had changed, and Jane had options. Her mother could offer experienced advice on whether or not to keep the baby.

But Rebel let out a little squeal of excitement and grinned with delight. "I'm going to be a grandmother. I'm going to be a grandmother."

Jane blanched. This was not the response she'd wanted to hear. Clearly she had not thought through going to her mother. Of course, she'd be happy about a first grandchild. And probably more thrilled when she discovered it was also Romeo's first grandchild. Jane groaned to herself. Now what did she do? How could she tell her mom that she wasn't sure she would be keeping the baby?

But Rebel was studying her, reading her, something she'd been able to do most of Jane's life. Rebel sank onto one of the stools, shoving aside her purse. "You do plan to keep the baby, don't you?"

Jane busied herself filling the teapot. "I—I don't know."

Her mom went very quiet for a long moment, and then she said, "Well, what about the baby's father? Does he want to keep the baby?"

Oh, God, Nick. Would he want the baby? She didn't know. Maybe. Probably. "I haven't told him."

"Well, darling, don't you think you should?"

"I only just found out myself last night, after work."

Her mother glanced toward the window. "That was twenty-four hours ago."

Jane exhaled. "I know."

Oh, man. This was her mother's and Nick's father's first grandchild. They were all going to weigh in on this decision once they found that out.

"Do you love the baby's father, Jane?"

"I—I . . ." How did she feel about Nick? That was just as confusing as the dilemma about the baby.

"Is he the young man we talked about the day we were looking for wedding attire?"

Jane nodded.

"Then you're still uncertain whether what you feel for him is lust or love."

"Oh, it's not love. I'm sure of that." Jane ignored the voice in her head asking how she could be so certain since she hadn't ever been in love. "But I can't stand what it will do to him if I choose not to have the baby."

Her mother studied her, then smiled. "I'm sure you'll figure it out and do the right thing."

"I need to talk to him, huh?"

"That's right, sweetheart."

But while driving to his loft, Jane discovered she

wasn't ready to face Nick. She needed a second opinion, a male perspective, and who better to give her advice about men than her dad? She called, and Eddie Wilson agreed to meet her at Big Sky Pie. Several of the tables were occupied with families having dessert. She was glad to find the end booth empty and slipped onto the seat to wait for her dad. She ordered coffee and pie à la mode for them both, though she doubted she could eat a bite, given her nerves.

Her dad arrived in his good old boy attire, jeans, shit-kicker boots, checkered shirt, and bolo tie. His idea of casual professional. He kissed her cheek and slid onto the bench seat across from her, his Old Spice aftershave giving her a sense of calm. He took her hands in his. "What's this all about, pumpkin?"

Jane had decided not to tell him about the baby for fear he'd have the same reaction her mom had had. What she wanted from him was an idea how she might expect Nick would react to the news. She kept her questions general, focusing on his view of how he felt discovering he was going to be a father.

"You have to remember, Janey, I was seventeen, captain of the football team, potential college scholarships ahead of me. I won't lie. It was a blow." He laughed. "But hell, it goes with the territory. Teenage boys are one big mass of raging hormones and testosterone. Logic, reason, good sense, none of that comes into the equation. Sports and getting laid. That's pretty much all they think about. Sadly, it can really get a fella's adulthood off on the wrong foot."

"Didn't you love Mom?"

He sighed. "Not the forever kind of love. We should've never given in to our baser instincts, probably wouldn't have if her mom hadn't died. That woman did not like me sniffing around your mom. She was right to be worried. I was a guy, and I pushed it and screwed up her dreams as well as mine. The only good thing to come out of it was you, baby. We never regretted you."

Jane knew that was true. She'd never had reason to doubt it, even if her parents hadn't been right for each other. The waitress brought their pie and coffee. Jane picked up her fork and poked it into the blueberry pie. "Dad, how do you know if you've met the right person?"

He dug into the food, filling his spoon with a huge bite of pie and ice cream. "I'm no expert on the subject. I can only speak from my own experiences. Your mom wanted me to be someone I wasn't, and I wanted the same from her. Don't ever hook up with someone who doesn't appreciate you as you are. The best partner is the one who loves you enough to let you be you. Vicky does that for me."

In that moment, Jane realized her dad was actually happy with her stepmother, had probably always been. She'd completely misread their relationship. She left feeling better, about her dad and Vicky, but dreading the conversation she needed to have with Nick.

Chapter Fourteen

As Jane drove to Nick's, her mind reeled back to the moment she'd seen the plus sign on the pregnancy stick, the moment realization struck, a 7.0 mega-shaker quaking through her. But now, she wondered why she'd been so stunned. Hadn't she told Nick that they'd had unprotected sex that first time? She shook her head. To think her only concern was an STD. This outcome was so contrary to what she'd envisioned for herself that she'd denied the possibility.

"When it comes to men, Janey, your mama is as flaky as the buttery crust on my blueberry pie." Jane swore, and muttered, "So much for all the 'I'll never be like my mother when I grow up. I won't make the same mistakes she made. I know the pitfalls, and I will avoid them.' Yeah, right."

For a smart, goal-oriented woman, she had majorly screwed up. Her life plan did not include complications like a husband or children. She enjoyed being single. No one to tell her what to do, how to do it, when to do it. No one to report to, her free time her own, and her only responsibilities those she chose. She didn't even have a pet, for God's sake.

Though she had been thinking about getting a cat.

Her heart picked up a beat as she turned onto Nick's street and spotted a light in the loft window. Music blasted from the Broken Spur across the street, and parking spots were at a premium. She found one two blocks down, locked the Jeep, and hurried to Nick's door, her nerves fraying with every beat of the brokenhearted country tune spilling through the saloon's swinging doors. An omen?

She hugged her purse to her chest, willing herself to breathe. How could she have allowed her body to dictate her decisions, to rob her of choices? She wanted to blame Nick, but seriously—safe sex was the responsibility of both willing participants. She could have provided condoms as easily as he. If she'd had any. Well, maybe the first time, she should have bought one since she'd come to his loft intending to sort of seduce him, but the second time…they hadn't known they'd be locked in the cold room, or that she'd be so cold, or that he'd be so irresistible…

Besides, by then, it was already too late. Oh, God, just thinking about Nick made her want him again.

She rang the bell. A moment later, his voice came over the intercom, and Jane found a lump in her throat the size of a golf ball. "Nick, it's me, Jane."

There was a long pause. She thought maybe he'd gone, walked away from the intercom. "Nick?"

He said nothing, just buzzed her in. The door closed behind her, the silence in the entry area muting all the saloon noise, wrapping her in an eerie quiet. She scrambled for the stairs, distrusting the shadowed corners, and hurried up. Nick waited on the landing, the open loft door spilling light along the upper hallway.

She slowed, trying to read him. He looked a little disheveled, hair mussed, jaw whiskered, a sunburned streak on the tip of his nose, and he was wearing those damned pajama bottoms and baggy T-shirt. Why did he always have to look so darned delicious? And why didn't he say something, like "Hi," or "Get out," or "What the hell do you want?" Something. Anything. Instead of checking her over like a bidder at a cattle auction assessing a prime side of beef. Maybe she shouldn't have worn such a short skirt.

"Are you going to invite me in or not?"

"Depends." He tipped his head, gave her a crooked smile, and drawled, "Am I going to regret it?"

That was a loaded question. Would he? She doubted that he'd jump for joy. More like run for the hills, but he had the right to know. "We need to talk."

"Oh, yeah? Why? Have you changed your mind about us?"

Her mouth was as dry as dust. "Something like that."

"That sounds...encouraging."

"Tell me that after I tell you why I'm here."

He frowned. "Okay, why don't you come on in?"

As she passed him, she realized he smelled like a brewery. "Have you been drinking?"

"Hell, yes. Dad's bachelor party. Fishing, drinking, too much sun, and too little you." He reached for her, but she scooted out of his reach.

This was a bad idea. How could she have this talk with him if he was drunk? But putting this off until the next day was not an option. She might lose her nerve altogether. "How about we get some coffee into you?"

"You're a real buzz-kill, you know?"

"You ain't seen nothin' yet, pal." She went to the kitchen area and filled the pot with water.

"Then show me..." He hitched a hip against the counter, staring at her as she put coffee grounds into the filter. His nearness caused her hand to tremble.

"It's not something I want to show you, but rather tell you. Something I need to tell you." She glanced at him and saw that the seriousness of her tone had finally registered.

"I know. You didn't mean it when you said you only wanted to be friends with benefits?" His grin was a sinful turn-on.

She willed her body to stop reacting to his every lure, but it was no use. If her body controlled her, she'd be toast whenever he looked at her. Hell, she was already toast. He was staring at her mouth, leaning in, aiming for a kiss. She pulled the glass coffeepot from beneath the spout too soon and dripping water sizzled on the burner. She filled a mug and thrust it into his hands. "Drink."

Nick startled. He looked into the cup as though seeing something alien, then at the coffeemaker. "This isn't even coffee yet. It's still percolating."

"Well...well, I need to talk to you before things get carried away."

"Then start talking 'cause things are already halfway to carried away."

She glanced at his pajama bottoms and blushed. "Nick, this is serious. As serious as it gets."

He indicated his condition with a nod of his head. "So is this."

"Could you get your mind"—and your body—"out of the bedroom for a moment?" Jane left the burbling coffee and walked to the seating area and sat in one of the armchairs.

Nick dumped his mug into the top of the coffeemaker and followed her. "What's going on, Pain?"

"Remember when you told me about how your parents ended up together?"

He looked disgusted as he sank onto the arm of the chair opposite her. "Is this about our parents again?"

"Yes, and no."

"Look, I know I wasn't for their remarriage at first, but I am now. My dad is happier than a kid on Christmas Day. I'm not going to do anything to spoil that, and I hope you're not either. In fact, I'm trying to make it up to your mom for whatever part I might have played in their breakup."

This was so unlike the Devil she knew that Jane was taken aback. Had she misjudged him? Given him no credit for growing up? Maybe so. She might even get to like this new Nick. And considering her mother was also happier than Jane had ever seen her, Jane made a promise to herself to be magnanimous toward Nick's dad. "This is not about our parents getting remarried."

"Then what?"

Oh, God, please give me the right words. But she didn't have anything that could soften the blow or the impact. It was what it was. "Nick, I'm pregnant. We're going to have a baby."

She might have shot him through with a bullet from his shocked, mouth-dropped expression.

"I know, it's your worst nightmare." *And mine.* "I mean, the same thing happened to your mother, to mine. Pregnant. Unwed." Not in love with the father of her child. And worse yet, Jane didn't want a child. A child would ruin her plans. Sure, other people managed to have children and careers—Andrea, for example—and managed to be great moms. But Jane wasn't just thinking of herself. She didn't want to bring a baby into the world who would be constantly shuffled between two parents. She had been that kid. Her heart ached at the thought that she could do that to a child of her own. "Say something, Nick."

"Oh, my God, I'm going to be a dad." His voice was filled with wonderment, not regret. Joy, not distress. His gaze sought hers, a smile lifting his lips. "This is the best news ever."

"What? Are you crazy?" Jane hadn't expected him to

have almost the same reaction as her mother. "I don't even know if I want to keep the baby."

"Are you kidding me? This is our child, Jane. Yours and mine. A miracle that came from our lovemaking. It was meant to be. How could you not want to keep this baby? My baby? Our baby. If our parents had chosen that option, neither you nor I would be here now. We deserved to live. So does our baby."

He was drunk. He wasn't supposed to make sense. But damn it all, he did.

"Jane, marry me. Let me give you and our baby everything you want."

"I want to go to school and work in France."

"Okay."

"What do you mean, okay? Your mother ran off and left you for her job, and you hated it. Would you want me to do the same to our child?"

"Absolutely not." He leaned toward her. "My job allows me to work from home, or from anywhere else that has Wi-Fi and Internet. I can be a—a househusband. The baby and I won't keep you from having your career or going to school or working in France. When you're ready for that transition, we'll go with you. Everywhere you are will be home for us."

Jane's throat constricted. She couldn't wrap her mind around this. Nick was offering her the moon and the stars. My God, this was every woman's dream proposal. He wasn't taking anything from her, but enhancing her life, solving this problem with the only solution to which she could see no downside. All that generosity, plus he was easy on the eyes and great in bed. What more could she want?

She ignored the little voice inside her screaming, "Love."

She loved Nick...like a friend, like a brother, like a sex buddy. Maybe one day it would develop into the forever kind of love, but she knew that wasn't what she felt now. On the other hand, what if it never happened? Then what? Would Nick default on the promises he'd just made her? She shouldn't ever forget he had a devilish side. "Do you promise, Nick, that when the time comes, you won't change your mind about living in France for two or three years?"

"I promise." He did the Scout's honor sign.

He looked sincere, but he'd been drinking. "I want it in writing."

He laughed. "I'll write it in blood if you insist."

"I faint at the sight of blood." She didn't really, but he didn't need to know that. At least not right now. "A legal document will do."

"First thing in the morning." He leaned into her. "Right after I buy you an engagement ring."

An engagement ring. Wow, this was really happening. She was going to marry the Tazmanian Devil. "When are we going to do this?"

"As soon as we can get the license and a judge. Or would you rather we eloped to Vegas? I know of a couple of chapels where Elvis officiates."

"I don't think my dad would appreciate my eloping." Though it might avoid some of the drama this was bound to stir up on the paternal side of her family. "He's always planned to give me away, despite my determination to never get married."

"Holy shit. Wait 'til I tell my dad." Nick let out a whoop and grabbed his cell phone. "He's going to be a father-in-law and a granddaddy in one fell swoop."

"No," Jane said, and Nick stilled.

"Why not?"

"Let's tell them together, tomorrow, after we see the lawyer and get the ring." She could only imagine how shocked Dad and Vicky and Gram were going to be, especially when they learned that it was Nick she was marrying.

"You think your dad might try to smash my face in when he finds out you're expecting my baby?"

"It's not out of the realm of possibilities."

That had Nick grinning again. "Vegas is sounding better by the minute."

"But our families and friends are here."

"It might not be the most comfortable wedding, given the family dynamics."

Nothing about this was comfortable. "All the more reason for a super-short engagement."

Nick nodded. "The shortest engagement on record. Guinness-World-Records short. I'm not giving you time to reconsider and back out."

"I can hardly back out. I'm the one having your baby."

"Our baby." Nick picked her up as though she weighed nothing.

Jane stopped resisting as he carried her to the bedroom, giving herself over to her body's needs and his, enjoying every scintillating second of their lovemaking.

But in the deep, dark hours of early morning, with Nick spooned against her, his breath warm against her neck, and contentment spread like a satin sheet over her, she heard the doubts whispering. Everything was moving so fast. Maybe too fast?

* * *

Nick stood at the back of the church, fidgeting. "Is my tie straight?"

Quint, his best man, eyed the bow tie. "Perfect."

"When are they going to start? Everyone we invited is present."

"Getting cold feet?"

"Hell no."

"Hey, watch your language. You're in a church, remember?"

The only church that had been available on such a short notice was this tiny secular chapel on the outskirts of town near Flathead Lake. The preacher was one of Andrea's uncles. Nick's dad was as thrilled as Jane's mother about the baby and impending grandparenthood. Jane's Gram was equally excited until she realized the baby's father was the son of *that* Italian, but Nick felt he'd won the Wilsons over when he asked Eddie for permission to marry his daughter and assured her family that, although the circumstances might seem like a shotgun wedding, nothing was farther from the truth.

Baby or no baby, Nick loved Jane. He'd marry her a hundred times over if he could. But the baby was the only reason she was marrying him. The realization stung, but not enough for him to walk away. Once she was his wife, the odds would increase that she'd eventually fall in love with him, wouldn't they?

The phone in his pocket vibrated, and he pulled it out wondering who had the bad timing. One of his customers? Thinking he should have turned his phone off, he realized he was holding Jane's phone, not his. She'd left it at his place last night, and he'd meant to return it this morning, but no one would let him see her, so he'd held on to it. He started to hit the shut down button, then realized she'd received a text from her doctor that said urgent. He debated for half a second, then opened the text. It read, *Good news. You are not pregnant.*

Nick felt his heart drop to his toes.

"Hey, are you okay?" Quint asked. "You're whiter than your shirt."

"Fine," he croaked. The sweet aroma of roses reached him, taking on a cloying, funereal odor, gagging him. This news changed nothing. Absolutely nothing. Did it? Would Jane go through with the wedding if she knew she wasn't having his baby? Nick thought he might hurl. He had to do the right thing. *Tell her.* Let her make the choice. *Now.* Before it was too late to turn back.

But as he struggled with the issue, the organ music began to play. Quint caught his arm. "It's show time, buddy. Have you got your vows?"

Nick absently patted his tuxedo pocket. "Right here. Memorized."

"I've got the rings. Let's do this thing."

The altar was decorated with huge bouquets of white roses, courtesy of the Flower Garden. Dean and Betty Gardener sat in a pew near the front of the chapel and were delighted to be among the limited number of wedding guests. Molly and Callee McCoy occupied the pew in front of them. Andrea and her sons were seated beside Molly and Callee. BiBi had arrived with Liam, and they chose to sit on the bride's side of the church. Jane's stepmother and grandmother were in the front pew, and Nick's dad sat in the front of his side of the church. Rebel was Jane's matron of honor.

Nick watched her come down the aisle alone and take her place beside him. Then the organ music escalated into the wedding march, everyone stood, and Jane and her father were coming toward him. Nick's heart squeezed at his first sight of her in her wedding gown, a long, satiny, strapless number in an off-white that gave her skin a creamy glow. Her bouncy hair peeked from beneath a lacy veil, red-gold curls framing her amazing aqua eyes. His chest ached for the love he felt. He was the luckiest man in the world. He wanted to shout it. But he was about to marry her under false pretenses. She didn't know. He needed to tell her.

But if he told her before the ceremony, she might walk out on him. The thought of coming this close to claiming her as his own, only to lose her, almost brought him to his knees.

Eddie Wilson handed his daughter to Nick and murmured, "Be the man she deserves."

Nick swallowed, guilt choking him.

He and Jane turned toward the preacher, who started out with the "Dearly beloved" stuff and then said, "If anyone present knows of any reason why this man and this woman should not be married, speak now or forever hold your peace."

An uncomfortable silence fell over the chapel, but no one spoke up. The preacher started to continue. Nick raised a hand. "Wait. Give me a minute."

Confusion and alarm filled Jane's eyes. "Nick, what are you doing?"

He leaned closer to her and whispered, "Your doctor texted. The blood test was negative."

She shook her head as if in denial, but then quickly seemed to catch on. "You mean, I'm not..."

"That's right. You're not. You don't have to go through with this ceremony if you don't want to." *But please want to.* He waited, feeling like an innocent man on death row with his last appeal, awaiting a judge's decision, his life on the line. His heart was hers for the breaking.

Her hesitation pounded home the truth. If she loved him, she wouldn't have hesitated. He'd lost the woman he loved, and the baby they'd already started to love, in one poorly timed text. Heartbreak and rage swept through Nick. Shaking, he kissed her cheek and said, "Have a nice life, Pain."

With that, he walked up the aisle and out the church door and disappeared.

Chapter Fifteen

～

It never got old. Coming into work in the wee hours of the morning and catching the scent of freshly baked pie that still lingered in the kitchen from the previous day's baking. Jane had expected it would be different this morning, though, and was surprised to find it unchanged, despite her whole world having shifted on its axis twice in the past ten days. Maybe the familiar would be good for her, pull her out of the doldrums. God knows, the weekend she'd taken off after the disaster in the chapel hadn't helped. One minute she'd been about to marry the Devil, about to embrace marriage as if she hadn't shied away from it her whole life, and the next, he was walking out on her.

Jane switched on all the lights, stowed her purse, and put on an apron. In the café, she started a pot of coffee, then returned to the kitchen and pulled out flour, parchment paper, rolling pins, and pie tins. How she wished she could take back that moment when Nick asked if she wanted to go on with the marriage ceremony, wished she had reacted differently to the news that she was not pregnant.

But her emotions had slammed into each other like freeway traffic on a foggy road, leaving her as confused as if she'd banged her head on a windshield. She went from stunned to relieved to disappointed to sad, sadder than she'd thought possible. The child she had never wanted had started to be so real that she'd begun to imagine a little boy with Nick's dimples and dark eyes, a little girl with her bouncy curls. She couldn't grasp the fact that there was not going to be a baby, or understand why that broke her heart so much.

She selected a mound of dough from the Sub-Zero, deciding to make cottage cheese pies, which required single crusts, opting for the comfort food without noting the correlation to her need for comfort. She floured a sheet of parchment paper and the rolling pin, then began rolling pie rounds. Her mind went back to Nick. Once she realized he was gone, really gone—not at his loft, not answering her calls, her texts—the oddest, most awful emptiness swept through Jane. She felt like she'd lost her best friend, like her mother must have felt after divorcing Romeo, like pies had been banned from the earth. She was in love with Nick. How could she finally understand that only after she'd lost him? And what could she do about it now? Especially since he wouldn't talk to her.

BiBi arrived, interrupting her dark musings, bustling

in all bright-eyed and as eager as a puppy, probably just as curious. Jane decided to beat her to the punch. "So are you and Liam dating?"

"Not exclusively, but we're having fun." BiBi slipped on an apron. "Is that coffee I smell? Oh, bless you. I'll bring you a cup, too."

Jane thanked her and then directed her to start stemming the blueberries she'd placed in the sink. BiBi worked without talking for ten minutes, a record for sure, then as Jane was putting the first cottage cheese pies into the oven, BiBi said, "Did you hear that Molly has Quint and Nick working on some secret project?"

Jane's pulse kicked up. "What?"

"They're in Los Angeles doing something or other. I couldn't get any details out of her, but it sounds exciting. She says she'll tell us all about it if it works out as she wants it to. Do you think she's maybe opening another pie shop in Hollywood? If so, I would be willing to transfer out there."

Molly McCoy was a Montana woman through and through. Jane could not imagine anyone less Hollywood. "It doesn't seem likely. She's barely launched Big Sky Pie. I think she'd consider branching out only if this shop proves to be a huge success financially, and then it would more than likely be in some other Montana town."

BiBi sighed. "I suppose that makes sense, but what could it be then?"

Jane shrugged. She hadn't a clue. "I guess we'll

have to wait until Molly wants to share the news. If there is any."

BiBi brought the stemmed, rinsed blueberries to the work counter in a large ceramic bowl. She set it down and gazed pointedly at Jane. "I'm going to stop dancing around this. Have you heard from him or not?"

Jane resisted the urge to dump the bowl on her assistant's tactless head. What didn't she get about being insensitive? "No."

"I shouldn't interfere but I can't stand to see you moping around like this. Why did you let that man get away? And what are you going to do to get him back?"

"He doesn't want me back."

BiBi rolled her eyes. "Have you been smoking weed?"

"No. He's probably out in Hollywood hooking up with a starlet or two."

"I'll grant you that women might be throwing themselves at him, especially if they catch sight of those dimples, but he doesn't have eyes for anyone but you. I know. I tried to get them onto me, if you recall."

Jane shook her head. She knew Nick was a player. He'd had a lot of relationships. "He was only marrying me because he thought I was having his baby."

"That is so not the case. Didn't you hear what happened when he went out with Andrea's girlfriends?"

"I heard her tell you they were smitten with him." *Who wouldn't be?*

"Well, you obviously didn't hear everything they had to say about him. They were smitten for the first five minutes. After that, all he talked about was some pastry chef named Jane. They both asked Andrea who the hell Jane was and what was so special about her."

Jane's hand stilled on the rolling pin. "Are you telling me the truth?"

"I swear on my dad's Daytime Emmys."

The ice around Jane's heart cracked wide open, spilling out a ray of hope. As soon as Molly showed up that morning, Jane took her aside. "I need a favor. A really big favor."

* * *

Tension played along Nick's nerve endings as he and Quint entered the pie shop to help Molly make the announcement to her staff. The aroma brought Jane's image like a slam to his heart. He considered backing out, letting Quint handle this, but Molly had insisted he be here and he didn't want to disappoint her. Or piss her off. She was turning out to be one of his best clients.

"Sounds like they're all in the kitchen," Quint said, heading straight for the coffee counter. "Want some?"

"Sure." He'd like a shot of whiskey in his, if one had been available, to boost his courage. "Black."

"I know."

They found the staff gathered around the work island and received afternoon greetings. To Nick's relief and disappointment, though, Jane was not among them. Had she gone home early to avoid him? Probably. Another fissure slid through the middle of his fractured heart.

Molly, dressed more appropriately for attending a church function than baking pies, gestured Quint and Nick onto the two stools beside her. In fact, Andrea, BiBi, and Callee also seemed more dressed up than usual. Probably for the big announcement.

Everyone settled down and all eyes turned toward Molly. It was hard to believe she'd had a triple bypass just three months ago. Even her hair looked healthier, the glow as red as the cherries she baked. Her eyes twinkled with excitement, drawing everyone in, as she said, "I spent a good deal of my recuperation watching TV, and I discovered most of my favorite game shows and dramas have been replaced by reality shows. Some of them are as addictive as soap operas used to be."

"I love reality shows," BiBi said.

Molly nodded. "One of my favorites is set in a cupcake shop and another has to do with cakes. After watching them for a few weeks, I got to thinking, why not a show set in a pie shop in Montana? Long story short, I ran the idea past Nick and Quint, and they agreed to check into it. They've just returned from Los Angeles after a two-week investigation into how to go about this, and I'm excited to tell you all, we have landed a contract to shoot a pilot for a reality show set in Big Sky Pie."

Andrea's mouth dropped open. "A reality show? With cameras following us everywhere?"

"Not everywhere," Molly said. "Just everywhere at the pie shop. Your personal life will still be off camera."

"OMG," BiBi said. "I'm going to be a reality TV star."

"Uh, BiBi," Quint said. "This is only a pilot. No network has picked it up yet. We don't know if anyone will. This is just the first step."

"When does the pilot start shooting?" Andrea asked, looking less convinced than BiBi that this was a great idea.

"Not until next month," Molly said. "And for now, this news stays among the six of us here and Jane. Don't tell anyone else. Not your parents, or friends, or boyfriends. Swear."

Everyone swore.

"Okay, then. Unless someone has something else they need to discuss, everyone is free to do what you should be doing."

As the others scrambled to their feet, Molly caught Nick's arm. "Would you take a look at something for me in the cold room? I think it might make a great addition to the blog."

"Sure." Nick slid off his stool and followed Molly down the hall to the cold room. He stepped back to let her enter first, but she insisted he go ahead of her. The second Nick was inside, the door slammed behind him and locked. He spun around. Molly was not there. "What the hell? Molly, is this some kind of joke? Quint?"

No one answered. He reached for his phone.

"Nick . . ."

Jane's voice stopped him. He pivoted. She stood not three feet away, wearing the sexy, curve-hugging black dress and leopard pumps she'd worn the first time he'd kissed her. Her bouncy hair shifted over her shoulders as she moved closer. His blood began to pump, heading south faster than robins in approaching winter. He scowled, unable to keep the anger from his voice. "What the hell is this?"

She smiled and blushed, fidgeting as though uncertain about where to start, what to say. "It's me, asking for a second chance."

"Excuse me?" He ran his hand through his hair. "A second chance for what?" *To humiliate me? To break my heart again?* He banged on the door. "Quint, let me out of here."

"Nick, please..."

"Fine. Say what you have to say and hurry up. It's cold in here."

She moved closer, ran her palms down his arms. His muscles tensed, and his breath lodged in his throat, but he didn't pull back, couldn't move if he tried.

She said, "I learned something this week. Love never shows up when you want it to. Usually it arrives when you least want it to, and even when you hope it never will."

She had his attention now. She touched his face. "I'm a planner. Have been all of my life. But I didn't plan on falling in love, especially with you, and I didn't recognize it when it happened, or that it had happened until you walked out of the chapel. Please tell me you forgive me and that you still love me."

Nick thought his knees might give out. He couldn't believe he was hearing this. "You love me?"

"More than baking pies."

That stunned him. "I thought you were only marrying me because of the baby."

"I thought that's why you were marrying me."

"We're a fine pair of fools."

"Nick, will you marry me? Right now? Right here at Big Sky Pie?"

Nick shook his head. "No."

Jane's stomach dipped. "No?"

"Not in this damned cold room."

"I can fix that." Jane drew out her cell phone, and a second later, Quint released them from their prison.

Jane led Nick into the café, which had been quickly decorated with flowers and balloons and held all the special guests who'd been at the chapel. Everyone cheered. Jane's dad gave her away again, warning Nick, "You stop the ceremony this time, Taziano, and you'll answer to me."

Nick promised that wouldn't happen. Dean pinned a carnation to Nick's shirt. Andrea added a veil to Jane's hair, and her mother gave her a bouquet. The wedding march issued from the kitchen CD player. Quint assured Nick, "I still have the rings."

The vows were exchanged without a hitch, and the pastor told Nick, "You may kiss your wife."

Nick had never heard sweeter words. Or tasted sweeter lips. He didn't think he could be happier. Champagne corks popped, and toasts were made. Romeo congratulated his son and new daughter-in-law. Eddie did the same. Quint toasted his mother's new venture into reality TV.

Nick decided to toast his dad and Rebel. "To the next soon-to-be-wed Tazianos."

But instead of his dad joining in, Romeo glanced at his fiancée. She nodded, then said, "We got married in Vegas before moving back to Kalispell. We decided nothing was going to come between us this time."

Laughter burst into the already joyous air. Nick handed Jane a flute of bubbly to toast their marriage. They clinked their glasses together, but before Jane could bring her glass to her mouth, a loud banging on the pie shop door startled everyone.

Molly opened the door, and a man rushed in, looked around the room, spied Jane, and said, "Stop. Don't drink that, Ms. Wilson."

"It's Mrs. Taziano now."

"Congratulations." He snatched the glass from Jane's hand, holding it out of her reach. As she protested, he slapped a bottle of pills into her hand. Nick stared at the bottle, then at Jane, who looked as confused as he felt, then at the man.

"Who is this guy?" Nick asked. "And what the hell is in that bottle?"

"He's my doctor," Jane said.

"It was a mix-up, you see." The doctor took a hefty gulp of champagne and then apologized profusely. "My receptionist switched phone numbers, sent the wrong text messages. I didn't know it until today when the other patient showed up to question her blood work results."

"Get to the point, Doctor," Molly said.

"Oh, sure." He took another gulp of champagne. "Those are prenatal vitamins. You are definitely pregnant, Jane. Congratulations."

Nick and Jane gaped at each other, and then happiness spread across Nick's face and through his happy heart. "We're going to have a baby, Jane."

"You are," the doctor assured him.

A cheer rocked through the pie shop as Nick grabbed his bride and hugged and kissed her. Happy tears spilled from Jane. Everyone was laughing and congratulating them. Jane looked up at her husband and smiled. Nick stared at her mouth, that wonderful, kissable mouth, and felt such joy he thought his heart might explode. "This, my love, is even more delicious than your sweet blueberry pie."

Big Sky Blueberry Pie

All-Butter Basic Crust

- 2½ cups all-purpose flour, plus extra for rolling
- 1 teaspoon salt
- 1 teaspoon sugar
- 1 cup (2 sticks or 8 ounces) unsalted butter, very cold, cut into ½-inch cubes
- 6 to 8 tablespoons ice water

Filling

- 6 cups fresh blueberries, stemmed and rinsed
- 1 tablespoon lemon juice
- ½ teaspoon lemon zest
- ¼ cup flour
- ½ cup sugar
- ¼ teaspoon cinnamon
- 2 tablespoons unsalted butter to dot on the top

Combine the flour, salt, and sugar in a food processor. Pulse until mixed. Add the cubed butter. Pulse 6 or 8 times, until the butter is pea-sized and the mixture looks like coarse meal. Next add ice water 1 tablespoon at a time. Pulse until the mixture just begins to clump. If you pinch some of the crumbly dough and it holds together, it's ready. If the dough doesn't hold together, add a little more water and pulse again. Caution: Too much water will make the crust tough.

Place the dough in a mound on a clean surface. Shape the dough mixture into two disks, one for the bottom crust, one for the top. Work the dough gently to form the disks. Don't overknead. You should be able to see flecks of butter in the dough. They will result in a flakier crust. Sprinkle a little flour around the disks. Wrap each disk in plastic wrap and refrigerate from 1 hour to 2 days.

Remove a crust disk from the refrigerator. Let it sit at room temperature for 5 to 10 minutes. This will soften it enough for easier rolling. On a lightly floured surface, roll out the dough to a 12-inch circle and about 1/8-inch thick. If the dough begins to stick to the surface below, then sprinkle some flour underneath. Carefully place the bottom crust into a 9-inch pie pan, pressing the dough gently into the bottom and sides of the pie pan. Trim excess dough, leaving about ½ inch more than the edge of the pie pan.

Gently mix all of the pie filling ingredients, except the butter, in a large bowl, and then put the filling into the chilled bottom crust and dot the top with the butter. Add the top crust and flute the edges. Place the pie into the refrigerator to chill for approximately 30 minutes. At the end of that time, remove the unbaked pie from the refrigerator, lightly brush the top crust with an egg wash made by whisking 1 large egg with 1 tablespoon of water, and then score the top crust with four cuts.

Preheat the oven to 425° F. Place the pie on the middle rack of the oven with a parchment paper– or Silpat-lined baking pan positioned on the lower rack to catch any filling that bubbles over. Bake for 20 minutes at 425° F. Reduce heat to 350° F and bake for 30 to 40 minutes more, or until juices are bubbling and have thickened.

Let cool completely before serving.

The last thing Ice Erikksen is looking for
in Kalispell, Montana, is to settle down.
But then he spots something delightful
in the pie shop—a sexy, single mama
with marriage on her mind...

Please see the next page

for a preview of

Delightful

Chapter One

❧

A couple of bites of my caramel apple pie and a man will look puppy-eyed at you," Molly McCoy, proprietor of Big Sky Pie, said. "A whole slice and he's liable to get down on one knee and offer a ring."

"Hah," Andrea Lovette, assistant manager of the Kalispell, Montana, pie shop, scoffed as she filled in the space for *Specialty of the Month* on the blackboard menu. "Oh, I'll give you that the pie smells like a little piece of heaven, but if all it took to snag a husband was a delightful mix of cinnamon, caramel, and green apple stuffed into a flaky, buttery crust, every marriage-minded female this side of Flathead Lake would be flocking to our doorstep in droves. And that is sadly not the case."

"I'm worried about the falling receipts, too, dear." Only Molly—red hair spiked, bright blue eyes full of smiles, wiping her hands on her apron as she surveyed the café and nodding approval—didn't look worried. Sunlight spilled into the room, glancing off the red tablecloths, beige walls, and accents of white and giving the space the warm ambience of a tearoom. "It's a known fact that restaurants generally lose money the first year or two after opening. I discussed that with my accountant before I applied for a building permit to re-model this place. So stop fretting."

"But we started out with such a bang." Andrea leaned back slightly on the stepladder and studied her handi-work, checking the lettering for spelling and readability. Satisfied, she descended the ladder, set it behind the front counter, and glanced around the empty café, each booth and table set and ready for customers. If only some would come in. She met Molly's gaze. "That huge chamber of commerce event at the mall, our grand open-ing gala, catering a couple of weddings and anniversary parties..."

Molly helped herself to tea. "Summer is always going to be a big season for us with all the tourists adding to the regular customers, but we have to expect business will dip once autumn arrives. Folks are busy gearing up for winter, or dieting before the holidays, or school's starting."

Seeking a diversion, Andrea glanced out the front windows. No cars in the parking lot, no one walking to-ward the door. She sighed. "I guess being a single mom of two, I'm always thinking of the budget's bottom line."

"You need something else to busy your mind. Like a man."

"Okay, there seems to be a theme to this conversation." *A theme about me, men, and marriage.* Andrea strode to the coffee counter, refilled her mug, and added a layer of caffeine to the anxiety in her stomach. "You aren't adding matchmaker to your résumé, are you?"

"No dear." Molly retied her apron around her middle, a middle that had shrunk considerably since her triple-bypass surgery four months ago. The heart-healthy diet was doing wonders for her figure, even if she grumbled constantly about "rabbit fodder." But now there was a mother-knows-all expression in her twinkly blue eyes. "I just noticed that wistful look you had at Nick and Jane's wedding this past summer. The same look that comes over you whenever Quint and Callee are in here together. You miss having a steady fella in your life."

Andrea breathed a little easier, tucking a strand of thick blond hair behind one ear, glad that there were no blind-date setups to cancel. On some level, she knew what Molly said was true, but she found herself denying it. "No. I don't."

"You do." Molly gave her a sad, indulgent smile. "Maybe it just takes one to know one, dear."

Andrea's heart clutched. Molly had lost her husband suddenly last winter, and his loss was still keen. She crossed to Molly and hugged her around the shoulders. "Donnie Lovette was no Jimmy McCoy. He was not the love of my life. I was young and stupid and should never have eloped with him or agreed to spend our first years on the rodeo circuit. My sons paid for those bad decisions." *Were still paying.*

"Ah, but then you wouldn't have had Logan and Lucas, and your life would be so much poorer for it."

Andrea couldn't dispute that. Her sons were the only two things she and Donnie had gotten right. "But if I had it to do over, I'd only consider marrying someone who would make a great father, someone steady that the boys and I could count on."

"You'd marry someone you didn't love?"

She shrugged. "If he was a great father, sure. Why not? Love is overrated."

Molly's eyebrows rose in disbelief. "You've seen proof to the contrary of that lately, right here in this very pie shop."

Andrea moaned to herself. "Yeah, well, I'm too busy for a serious relationship."

Molly laughed. "Love doesn't work like that. It's inconvenient. Messy. It comes along when you least expect it, or aren't looking for it, or really can't see how to fit it into your life."

That's a scary notion. Was it true? Andrea wouldn't know. What she thought was love when she married Donnie had more likely been raging teenage hormones. She'd never met a guy who'd made her feel whatever it was she saw in Callee's and Jane's eyes. She probably never would, given her weakness.

When it came to the opposite sex, her radar zeroed in on bad boys as if it were hardwired into her genes. She couldn't help herself. Line up a wall of eligible husband-types, toss in a confirmed bachelor, blindfold her, and she would chose the one-night-stand guy. Every. Single.

Time. It was her fatal flaw, the thing she would change about herself, if she could. That thing she could never tell Molly.

"You know, this is just the kind of conversation that would be great on our reality show," Molly said, sipping her tea with the innocence of the pope.

Andrea winced. This past summer, without bothering to first okay it with her staff, Molly had contracted with a Los Angeles production team for a pilot to be shot and shopped to the networks. Filming was supposed to commence by the end of this week. Even though the staff voted to go forward with the pilot, the closer the time came for shooting to start, the more misgivings Andrea had.

And the giddier Molly became. "I can't wait for the camera crew to show up."

Andrea could wait. She foresaw nothing but chaos and disaster in this undertaking. There was too much potential for things to go wrong. Close-the-shop wrong. "I have some serious reservations about the reality show. This is a small town. The bulk of our customers are people we know."

"Don't you see? That's the beauty of it. They'll tell their friends and family to watch the show. It will up our viewers and our ratings."

Andrea wondered why Molly couldn't see the pitfalls. The downside. "We'll become instant celebrities. The public will feel as if they know us personally. We'll have no buffer between them and us. Anything we say on the show is going to be out there, reviewed, dissected, analyzed. Everyone will be gossiping about us."

Molly's grin widened. "Of course they will. And they'll be coming in for pie."

"But have you seen how cutthroat shows like *Project Runway* and *Survivor* can be?"

Molly shook her head, giving a dismissive wave of her hand. "Those shows are contests. We're a family here. We'll be more like...the Kardashians."

Every bad consequence Andrea had ever imagined bounced through her mind.

"Besides, dear," Molly said, "we need the exposure to get folks back in here on a more regular basis. That will help the bottom line you're so anxious about. I'm counting on it to put us back in the black."

This shot down every objection that had occurred to Andrea. Molly was more concerned about the downturn in business than she was letting on. Andrea understood on a very basic level. Sometimes you had to do whatever it took to take care of your child, and to Molly, this pie shop was like a child. "All right, then. I promise I'll do my best to ensure the pilot is as entertaining as ...*The Real Housewives of Kalispell*."

Molly's brows arched. "There is no such show. Oh, ha. I see. That's funny." They laughed. Then a familiar, determined gleam returned to Molly's eye. "Now let's work on getting you a husband. Hmm. Who would make a good candidate?"

"Oh, no you don't." Andrea raised her palms to ward off the very notion.

"Okay. I'll have to think on it anyway." Humming, Molly retreated to the kitchen.

Five minutes later, the bell over the door sounded, and Andrea turned toward it in anticipation of customers, but it was only Suzilynn, their part-time counter help, arriving after school. The pert brunette, whose ponytail reached to her waist, had a friendly demeanor, did as she was told, but was not a self-starter. Her eyes popped wide behind wire-rimmed glasses. "OMG. It smells like my grandpa's apple orchard in here, only a gazillion times sweeter."

"Molly's newest recipe."

"Maybe we should prop open the door to lure in some customers. This place is deader than my cell phone."

"It's early yet," Andrea said, trying to reassure herself as much as to counter any bad vibes that statement conjured.

"If Ms. McCoy would play rap music instead of country, I could get my friends to come in after school."

Andrea bit her tongue to keep from reminding the girl that Big Sky Pie was a pie shop, not a teenager hangout. "Or maybe you could suggest they bring in their families for dessert after dinner."

Suzilynn's mouth puckered as if it were full of vinegar. "Their families?"

Andrea gave up, feeling old for not relating to this teenager. Not that long ago, she'd been a teen, right? "Until someone comes in, you can keep busy refilling the sugar holders. I have to make a couple of phone calls."

"If someone does come in, should I get you?" Suzilynn pushed her glasses up her nose.

"Not unless it's a stampede. Just take orders and serve the desserts." Andrea stifled her frustration. Suzilynn was capable of handling the café alone as long as there were no more than two tables of customers at the same time. Andrea seriously doubted that would be a problem today.

As Andrea stepped into the kitchen, a sorrowful country tune issued from the CD player. The kitchen staff was gone, the last of the day's pies were cooling on the racks, and Molly was wiping down the work area to ready it for tomorrow, singing along, making up words she didn't know. Her voice off-key. Sunlight shone in through the row of windows at the back wall and glinted off the stainless steel appliances. The cabinets were French Country, creamy and soothing, the large island workstation a solid slab of marble, its consistently cold surface the best for rolling pie dough.

Andrea made her calls, then came back out to find Molly finishing up. Molly handed her two pies. "These need to go out front. And I'm heading home."

"See you tomorrow." Andrea carried two pies to the display cases in the café. As she settled them onto a glass refrigerator shelf, she noted that in her absence a couple of men had arrived. *Good.* They sat in the middle of the three booths, conversing in low tones, viewing something on an iPad. The baby-faced one didn't seem much older than Suzilynn, a lanky, pink-cheeked kid, all legs and arms he had yet to grow into. The other guy was shorter, but well built, and surprisingly tan for someone with natural red hair. They were halfway through the specialty dessert à la mode.

Suzilynn had served them without mishap, Andrea was glad to see. Maybe all the girl needed was some confidence-building encouragement. She made a note to herself to offer praise whenever she could. She motioned for Suzilynn to see if the men needed more coffee. Suzilynn blushed, glanced at Baby Face, and caught his eye. His flirty, puppy-dog grin brought to mind Molly's words about the caramel apple pie.

Andrea shook her head, smiling to herself, and then she realized the redhead had focused on her. He said something she couldn't hear to his companion, and then both guys were glancing at her like they were auditioning the future mother of their children.

Andrea's spine stiffened. *As if.* Molly was wrong. She didn't need or want a husband. A man couldn't define her life or make it better. In fact, given her one and only foray into that not-so-happy state of matrimony, she'd rather avoid it forever. But was that fair to her two little boys? Mommy-guilt fell over her like a wet blanket. They had no man in their lives, no father figure, and there were just some roles a mom and grandma couldn't fulfill. For their sakes, shouldn't she try to find a guy who would make a wonderful stepfather? Didn't she owe them that?

Of course she did.

The bell over the café door jangled, announcing more customers, and before she could even glance up to greet the new arrivals, her bad-boy antennae began to twitch.

A moment later, he filled the doorway, tall, blond, tan, with mirrored aviators and an unconscious swagger. Her knees went weak. *God help me.* He wore Harley boots, torn jeans, a leather jacket, and an I-don't-give-a shit-about-anything attitude. Exactly her type. *Be still, my heart.* But that disobedient organ boogied inside her chest like a drunken line dancer, her pulse thrumming to the beat of an erotic guitar.

She braced herself and carried a menu to his table near the café's bay windows. "Welcome to Big Sky Pie. May I get you something to drink?"

"Depends," he said in a drawl that rivaled Sam Elliott's gravelly voice. He lifted his face, the lenses hiding his eyes. "What are you offering?"

Tingles rocked through Andrea, and she almost responded, "My body," but swallowed the words. "We have milk, coffee, espresso, tea, and water."

"Espresso." He rattled off some concoction with five ingredients.

Andrea laughed. "This isn't Starbucks. Our espresso is the basic brew."

"Then basic it is." His smile flashed teeth that were brighter than the porcelain sink in her apartment bathroom. Her gaze fell to his hands. No wedding ring. Not that that meant a thing. His kind never wore rings. She'd bet he was on a road trip, out for a good time with any and every female who crossed his path. No strings attached. Again, exactly her usual choice in lovers.

She swallowed hard as thoughts of making love with this man began stirring sensuous images and heating her blood. She turned to get his drink, but he stopped her. "Andrea?"

She blinked, startled that he knew her name. Were those mirrored aviators hiding the eyes of a guy she actually knew? Not possible. She would remember someone this hot. Then she caught her reflection in the mirrored glasses, her teal sweater...her name tag. "Yes?"

"What is that delightful scent?"

"It's the special of the month, caramel apple pie." She pointed toward the chalkboard menu, debating whether or not to shake some of his cockiness by telling him what Molly thought men would do after eating one bite of this pie. She smiled to herself but, in the end, decided against it. He'd probably take off running, and they needed his business. "It tastes even better than it smells."

"I'm sure it does." He shared a crooked, sexy-as-hell grin. "But I meant your perfume."

Andrea rolled her eyes. Seriously? Did this line actually work for him? Hell—considering the sex appeal radiating off him—probably any line worked. "How could you smell anything but the yummy aromas coming from our kitchen?"

"I have a very discerning nose."

"I see." More likely she'd dumped on too much fragrance that morning in her haste to get the boys to school.

"It's Chanel, right?"

This brought her up short. Maybe he wasn't a low-brow Neanderthal after all. Most of the guys she dated couldn't decipher cologne from air freshener. The scent she wore was an old one, the bottle given to her mother and regifted to Andrea. Andrea seldom spent money on herself and never for luxury items like expensive perfume. The boys' needs came first. Always. "What are you? A perfume salesman?"

He chuckled and leaned back in the chair, looking her up and down. "No one's ever called me that before."

A slew of things he probably had been called popped to mind and made her smile. His corresponding grin said he'd like to eat her up, and her body responded with a "Hell, yes!" Rattled, she escaped to the coffee bar for his espresso.

Suzilynn pushed her glasses up her nose and whispered, "He's hot...for an old guy."

Hot and a half, Andrea thought, but acted as if she hadn't really noticed his eye-candy delightfulness. "You think?"

"Yeah, I think. Who is he?"

A slick, smart-ass, Donnie Lovette clone. She shrugged. "Dunno. Some Harley Cowboy, just passing through."

"Really?" Suzilynn's eyebrows rose above the frame of her glasses. "Then how come he's taking photos of the café and everything?"

Andrea glanced toward Mirrored Aviators and received another heart jolt. "I didn't see a camera."

"He was using his phone and texting." Suzilynn's eyes rounded, a sure sign her imagination was about to run wild. "I bet he's some spy, checking out the competition."

"I doubt it." She dismissed the teenager's ridiculous suggestion and turned back to the espresso machine, reaching for his cup. But what if Suzilynn was on to something? Andrea shifted around quickly and caught him lowering his cell. A squiggle of unease wound through her. Could he be here scouting out this shop with plans to open something similar down the street in an attempt to run Molly out of business? On the surface, the idea seemed ludicrous, but given that receipts were dropping by the day, she couldn't shake it off. They were barely covering expenses.

"I'll find out." Suzilynn started toward Mirrored Aviators.

"No." Andrea caught her by the arm. "You can't just ask him."

"Why not?" The teenager gaped at her.

Andrea handed Suzilynn the espresso cup. "Take him this and get his pie order. And that's all."

Suzilynn was back a minute later. "He wants the special à la mode, but he wants you to deliver it."

Of course he does. She plated a slice of the caramel apple pie, heated it, then topped it with a scoop of cinnamon ice cream. The aroma snaked into her like erotic incense. Too bad its magical powers didn't include making a man tell the truth. She carried the dessert to his table.

She meant to ask if he needed anything else, but heard herself saying, "I know what you're doing."

"You do?" He seemed amused by the statement. "What gave me away?"

She raked a smoldering gaze the length of him, hoping to make him squirm. Like he'd made her squirm. "The way you're dressed, for one thing."

He glanced at his attire, then at her. "I don't get the connection."

"Oh, you get it."

"I do?"

The more amused he became, the more her anger spiked. "If you do anything to hurt Molly McCoy or this business, you'll have me to answer to."

He made a rumbling noise that sounded like suppressed laughter and that sparked hot shivers through her.

He said, "In that case, I won't do that."

"Make sure you don't."

He lifted his phone and snapped a photo of her. Andrea reared back, lost her balance, grabbed at air, and caught the tablecloth. As she pitched bottom-first to the floor, she watched the pie à la mode jump, then take flight, and drop into Mirrored Aviators' lap, the dish landing at his boots with a clatter. He swore, leaped from his chair, and cried, "Cut! Did you get that, Berg?"

"Of course I did." The redheaded dude slipped from the booth. "Wait 'til you see the footage. It's amazing."

Andrea, legs askew, skirt hiked up her thighs, realized she was giving these guys more than a little shot of her unmentionables. She scrambled to her feet, resisting the urge to rub her sore behind. "What the hell are you talking about?"

As Mirrored Aviators swiped at the front of his pants with a damp tea towel provided by Suzilynn, Berg pointed to the shelf beneath the chalk blackboard. Andrea's eyes widened. A camera. And another beside the cash register. Why had Suzilynn allowed that? She spun toward her counter girl to ask, but the teenager was cleaning up the mess and Baby Face was helping. Flirty glances and giggles passed between them. It was all the answer Andrea needed. He'd diverted Suzilynn so "Berg" could position the cameras.

Andrea's hands landed on her hips, murder filling her heart. She spun on Mirrored Aviators. "Who are you?"

He grinned and extended his card. "Ice Erikksen. My partner, Bobby Bergman. Ice Berg Productions. We're in charge of making the pilot for the reality show. And thanks to you, Andrea, we just got a sweet opening sequence."

THE DISH

Where Authors Give You the Inside Scoop

♥ ♥ ♥ ♥ ♥ ♥ ♥ ♥ ♥ ♥ ♥ ♥ ♥ ♥ ♥

From the desk of Debbie Mason

Dear Reader,

While reading CHRISTMAS IN JULY one last time before sending it off to my editor, I had an "oops, I did it again" moment. In the first book in the series, *The Trouble with Christmas*, there's a scene where Madison, the heroine, senses her late mother's presence. In this book, our heroine, Grace, receives a message from her sister through her son. Grace has spent years blaming herself for her sister's death, and while there's an incident in the book that alleviates her guilt, I felt she needed the opportunity to tell her sister she loved her. Maybe if I didn't believe our departed loved ones could communicate with us in some way, I would have done this another way. But I do, and here's why.

My dad was movie-star handsome and had this amazing dimple in his chin. He was everything a little girl could wish for in a father. But he wasn't my biological father; he was the father of my heart. He came into my life when I was nine years old. That first year, I dreamed about him a lot. The dreams were very real, and all the same. I'd be outside and see a man from behind and call out to him. He'd turn around, and it would be my dad.

I always said the same thing: "You're here. I knew you weren't gone." Almost a year to the day of his passing, my dad appeared in my dream surrounded by shadowy figures who he introduced to me by name. He told me that he was okay, that he was happy. It was his way, I think, of helping me let him go.

I didn't dream of him again until sixteen months ago when we were awaiting the birth of our first grandchild. I "woke up" to see him sitting at the end of my bed. I told him how happy I was that he'd be there for the arrival of his great grandchild. He said of course he would be. He wouldn't be anywhere else.

A week later, my daughter gave birth to a beautiful baby girl. When I saw my granddaughter for the first time, I started to cry. She had my dad's dimple. No one on my son-in-law's side, or ours, has a dimple in their chin. He used to tell us the angels gave it to him, and we like to think he gave our granddaughter hers as proof that he's still with us.

So now you know why including that scene was important not only to Grace, but to me. Life really is full of small miracles and magic. And I hope you experience some of that magic as you follow Grace and Jack on their journey to happy-ever-after.

Debbie Macomber

♥ ♥ ♥ ♥ ♥ ♥ ♥ ♥ ♥ ♥ ♥ ♥ ♥

From the desk of Kristen Ashley

Dear Reader,

Usually, inspiration for books comes to me in a variety of ways. It could be a man I see (anywhere), a movie, a song, the unusual workers in a bookstore.

With SWEET DREAMS, it was an idea.

And that idea was, I wanted to take a hero who is, on the whole, totally unlikable, and make him lovable.

Enter Tatum Jackson, and when I say that, I mean *enter Tatum Jackson*. He came to me completely with a *kapow!* I could conjure him in my head, hear him talk, see the way he moved and how his clothes hung on him, feel his frustration with his life. I also knew his messed-up history.

And I could *not* wait to get stuck into this man.

I mean, here's a guy who is gorgeous, but he's got a foul temper, says nasty things when he's angry, and he's not exactly father of the year.

He had something terrible happen to him to derail his life and he didn't handle that very well, making mistake after mistake in a vicious cycle he pretty much had no intention of ending. He had a woman in his life he knew was a liar, a cheat, and no good for anyone and he was so stuck in the muck of his life that he didn't get shot of her.

Enter Lauren Grahame, who also came to me like a shot. As with Tate, everything about Lauren slammed into my head, perhaps most especially her feelings, the disillusionment she has with life, how she feels lost and really has no intention of getting found.

In fact, I don't think with any of my books I've ever had two characters who I knew so thoroughly before I started to tell their story.

And thus, I got lost in it.

I tend to be obsessive about my storytelling but this was an extreme. Once Lauren and Tate came to me, everything about Carnal, Colorado, filled my head just like the hero and heroine did. I can see Main Street, Bubba's Bar, Tate's house. I know the secondary characters as absolutely as I know the main characters. The entirety of the town, the people, and the story became a strange kind of real in my head, even if I didn't know how the story was going to play out. Indeed, I had no idea if I could pull it off, making an unlikable man lovable.

But I fell in love with Tate very quickly. The attraction he has for Lauren growing into devotion. The actions that speak much louder than words. I so enjoyed watching Lauren pull Tate out of the muck of his life, even if nothing changes except the fact that he has a woman in it that he loves, who is good to him, who feeds the muscle, the bone, the soul. Just as I enjoyed watching Tate guide Lauren out of her disillusionment and offer her something special.

I hope it happens to me again someday that characters like this inhabit my head so completely, and I hope it happens time and again.

But Tate and Lauren being the first, they'll always hold a special place in my heart, and live on in my head.

Happily,

Kristen Ashley

♥ ♥ ♥ ♥ ♥ ♥ ♥ ♥ ♥ ♥ ♥ ♥ ♥ ♥ ♥ ♥

From the desk of Rebecca Zanetti

Dear Reader,

I'm the oldest of three girls, and my husband is the oldest of three boys, so we grew up watching out for our siblings. Now that we're all adults, they look out for us, too. While my sisters and I may have argued with one another as kids, we instantly banded together if anybody tried to mess with one of us. My youngest sister topped out at an even five feet tall, yet she's the fiercest of us all, and she loses her impressive temper quite quickly if someone isn't nice to me.

I think one of the reasons I enjoyed writing Matt's story in SWEET REVENGE is because he's the eldest of the Dean brothers, and as such, he feels responsible for them. Add in a dangerous military organization trying to harm them, and his duties go far beyond that of a normal sibling. It was fun to watch Matt try to order his brothers around and keep them safe, while all they want to do is provide backup for him and ensure his safety.

There's something about being the oldest kid that forces us to push ourselves when we shouldn't. When our siblings would step back and relax, we often push forward just out of sheer stubbornness. I don't know why, and it's sometimes a mistake. Trust me.

SWEET REVENGE was written in several locations, most notably in the hospital and on airplanes. Sometimes

I take on a bit too much, so when I discovered I needed a couple of surgeries (nothing major), I figured I'd just do them on the same day. Why not? So I had two surgeries in one day and had to spend a few days in the hospital recuperating.

With my laptop, of course.

There's not a lot to do in the hospital but drink milkshakes and write, so it was quite effective. Then, instead of going home and taking it easy, I flew across the country to a conference and big book signing. Of course, I was still in pain, but I ignored it.

Bad idea.

Two weeks after that, I once again flew across the country for a book signing and conference. Yes, I was still tired, but I kept on going.

Yet another bad idea.

Then I returned home and immediately headed back to work as a college professor at the beginning of the semester.

Not a great idea.

Are you seeing a trend here? I pushed myself too hard, and all of a sudden, my body said... *you're done.* Completely done. I became sick, and after a bunch of tests, it appeared I'd just taken on too much. So at the end of the semester, I resigned as a professor and took up writing full time. And yoga. And eating healthy and relaxing.

Life is great, and it's meant to be savored and not rushed through—even for us oldest siblings. I learned a very valuable life lesson while writing SWEET REVENGE, and I'll always have fond memories of this book.

I truly hope you enjoy Matt and Laney's story, and

don't forget to take a deep breath and enjoy the moment.
It's definitely worth it!

Happy reading!

Rebecca Zanetti

RebeccaZanetti.com
Twitter @RebeccaZanetti
Facebook.com

♥ ♥ ♥ ♥ ♥ ♥ ♥ ♥ ♥ ♥ ♥ ♥ ♥ ♥ ♥

From the desk of Shannon Richard

Dear Reader,

When it comes to the little town of Mirabelle, Florida,
Grace King was actually the first character who revealed
herself to me, which I find odd as she's the heroine in the
second book. I knew from the beginning she was going
to be a tiny little thing with blond hair and blue eyes; I
knew she'd lost her mother at a young age and that she
was never going to have known her father; and I knew
she was going to be feisty and strong.

Jaxson Anderson was a different story. He didn't
reveal himself to me until he literally walked onto
the page in *Undone*. I also didn't know about Jax and
Grace's future relationship until they got into an argument at the beach. As soon as I figured out they were
going to end up together, my mind took off and I started

plotting everything out, which was a little inconvenient as I wasn't even a third of the way through writing the first book.

Jax is a complicated fella. He's had to deal with a lot in his life, and because of his past he doesn't think he's good enough for Grace. Jax has most definitely put her on a pedestal, which is made pretty evident by his nickname for her. He calls her Princess, but not in a derogatory way. He doesn't find her to be spoiled or bratty. Far from it. He thinks that she should be cherished and that she's worth *everything*, especially to him. I try to capture this in the prologue, which takes place a good eighteen years before UNDENIABLE starts. Grace is this little six-year-old who is being bullied on the playground, and Jax is her white knight in scuffed-up sneakers.

Jax has been in Grace's life from the day she was brought home from the hospital over twenty-four years ago. He's watched her grow up into the beautiful and brave woman that she is, and though he's always loved her (even if he's chosen not to accept it), it's hard for him think that he can be with her. Jax's struggles were heartbreaking for me to write, and it was especially heartbreaking to put Grace through it, but this was their story and I had to stay true to them. Readers shouldn't fear with UNDENIABLE, though, because I like my happily-ever-after endings and Grace and Jax definitely get theirs. I hope readers enjoy the journey.

Cheers,

From the desk of Stacy Henrie

Dear Reader,

I remember the moment HOPE AT DAWN, Book 1 in my Of Love and War series (on sale now), was born into existence. I was sitting in a quiet, empty hallway at a writers' conference contemplating how to turn my single World War I story idea, about Livy Campbell's brother, into more than one book. Then, in typical fashion, Livy marched forward in my mind, eager to have her story told first.

As I pondered Livy and the backdrop of the story—America's involvement in WWI—I knew having her fall in love with a German-American would provide inherent conflict. What I didn't know then was the intense prejudice and persecution she and Friedrick Wagner would face to be together, in a country ripe with suspicion toward anyone with German ties. The more I researched the German-American experience during WWI, the more I discovered their private war here on American soil—not against soldiers, but neighbors against neighbors, citizens against citizens.

A young woman with aspirations of being a teacher, Livy Campbell knows little of the persecution being heaped upon the German-Americans across the country, let alone in the county north of hers. More than anything, she feels the effects of the war overseas through the absence of her older brothers in France, the alcohol troubles of her wounded soldier boyfriend, and the disruption of her studies at college. When she applies for a teaching job in hopes of escaping the war, Livy doesn't realize she's simply traded one set of troubles for another, especially when she finds herself attracted to the school's handsome handyman, German-American Friedrick Wagner.

Born in America to German immigrant parents, Friedrick Wagner believes himself to be as American as anyone else in his small town of Hilden, Iowa. But the war with Germany changes all that. Suddenly viewed as a potential enemy, Friedrick seeks to protect his family from the rising tide of injustice aimed at his fellow German-Americans. Protecting the beautiful new teacher, Livy Campbell, comes as second nature to Friedrick. But when he finds himself falling in love with her, he fears the war, both at home and abroad, will never allow them to be together.

I thoroughly enjoyed writing Livy and Friedrick's love story and the odds they must overcome for each other. This is truly a tale of "love conquers all" and the power of hope and courage during a dark time in history. My hope is you will fall in love with the Campbell family through this series, as I have, as you experience their triumphs and struggles during the Great War.

Happy reading!

Stacy Henrie

♥ ♥ ♥ ♥ ♥ ♥ ♥ ♥ ♥ ♥ ♥ ♥ ♥ ♥ ♥ ♥

From the desk of Adrianne Lee

Dear Reader,

Conflict, conflict, conflict. Every good story needs it. It heightens sexual tension and keeps you guessing whether a couple will actually be able to work through those serious—and even not so serious—issues and obstacles to find that happily-ever-after ending.

I admit to a little vanity when one of my daughters once said, "Mom, in other romances I always know the couple will get together early in the book, but I'm never sure in yours until the very end." High praise and higher expectations for any writer to live up to. It is, at least, what I strive for with every love story I write.

Story plotting starts with conflict. I already knew that Jane Wilson, Big Sky Pie's new pastry chef, was going to fall in love with Nick Taziano, the sexy guy doing the promotion for the pie shop, but when I first conceived the idea that these two would be lovers in DELICIOUS, I didn't realize they were a reunion couple.

A reunion couple is a pair who was involved in the past and broke up due to unresolved conflicts. This is what I call a "built-in" conflict. It's one of my favorites to write. When the story opens, something has happened that involves this couple on a personal level, causing them to come face-to-face to deal with it. This is when they finally admit to themselves that they still have feelings for each other, feelings neither wants to feel or act on, no matter how compelling. The more they try to suppress the attraction, the stronger it becomes.

In DELICIOUS, Jane and Nick haven't seen each other since they were kids, since his father and her mother married. Jane blames Nick's dad for breaking up her parents' marriage. Nick resents Jane's mom for coming between his father and him. Jane called Nick the Tazmanian Devil. Nick called her Jane the Pain. They were thrilled when the marriage fell apart after a year.

Now many years later, their parents are reuniting, something Jane and Nick view as a bigger mistake than the first marriage. Their decision to try and stop the wedding, however, leads to one accidental, delicious kiss, and a sizzling attraction that is as irresistible as Jane's blueberry pies.

I hope you'll enjoy DELICIOUS, the second book in my Big Sky Pie series. All of the stories are set in northwest Montana near Glacier Park, an area where I vacationed every summer for over thirty years. Each of the books is about someone connected with the pie shop in one way or another and contains a different delicious pie recipe. So come join the folks of Kalispell at the little pie shop on Center Street, right across from the mall, for some of the best pie you'll ever taste, and a healthy helping of romance.

Adrianne Lee

From the desk of Jessica Lemmon

Dear Reader,

A *quiz:* What do you get when you put a millionaire who avoids romantic relationships in the same house with a determined-to-stay-single woman who crushed on him sixteen years ago?

If you answered *unstoppable attraction*, you'd be right.

In THE MILLIONAIRE AFFAIR, I paired a hero who cages and controls his emotions with a heroine who feels way too much, way too soon. Kimber Reynolds is determined to have a fling—to love and leave Landon Downey, if for only two reasons: (1) She's wanted to kiss the eldest Downey brother since she was a teen, and (2) to prove to herself that she can have a shallow relationship that ends amicably instead of one that's long, drawn-out, and destined to end badly.

When Landon's six-year-old nephew, Lyon, and a huge account for his advertising agency come crashing into his life, Landon needs help. Lucky for him (and us!) his sister offers the perfect solution: her friend, Kimber, can be his live-in nanny for the week.

The most difficult part about writing Landon was letting him deal with his past on *his terms* and watching him falter. Here is a guy who makes rules, follows them, and remains stoic...to his own detriment. Despite those qualities, Landon, from a loving, close family, can't help caring for Kimber. Even when they're working down a list of "extracurricular activities" in the bedroom, Landon puts Kimber's needs before his own.

These two may have stumbled into an arrangement, but when Fate tosses them a wild card, they both step up—and step closer—to the one thing they were sure they didn't want... *forever.*

I *love* this book. Maybe because of how much I wrestled with Landon and Kimber's story before getting it right. The three of us had growing pains, but I finally found their truth, and I'm *so* excited to share their story with you. If Landon and Kimber win your heart like they won mine, be sure to let me know. You can email me at jessica@jessicalemmon.com, tweet me @lemmony, and "like" my Facebook page at www.facebook.com/authorjessicalemmon.

Happy reading!

Jessica Lemmon

www.jessicalemmon.com